UNFIT

UNFIT

Ariana Harwicz

translated from the Spanish
by Jessie Mendez Sayer

A NEW DIRECTIONS
PAPERBOOK ORIGINAL

Originally published as *Perder el juicio* by Anagrama in 2024
Published by arrangement with Gaeb & Eggers Literary Agency, Berlin

First published by New Directions in 2025 as NDP1649
Manufactured in the United States of America

Library of Congress Cataloging-in-Publication Data
Names: Harwicz, Ariana, 1977- author | Sayer, Jessie Mendez translator
Title: Unfit / Ariana Harwicz ;
translated from the Spanish by Jessie Mendez Sayer.
Other titles: Perder el juicio. English
Description: New York : New Directions Publishing, 2025. |
"A New Directions paperbook original."
Identifiers: LCCN 2025029507 | ISBN 9780811238892 paperback |
ISBN 9780811238908 ebook
Subjects: LCGFT: Fiction | Novels
Classification: LCC PQ7798.418.A79 P4713 2025 |
DDC 863/.7—dc23/eng/20250627
LC record available at https://lccn.loc.gov/2025029507

2 4 6 8 10 9 7 5 3 1

New Directions Books are published for James Laughlin
by New Directions Publishing Corporation
80 Eighth Avenue, New York 10011

For Sofia T.
Delphine Jubillard
Alexia Fuillot
Vanina Fonseca

For Lisa
for answering my urgent call
in the middle of a field of sunflowers

UNFIT

Serial killers were asked what they felt the first time, if the act of murder had been chilling. Not really, to tell you the truth, they replied. You can watch security camera footage from bars and restaurants where killers and kidnappers of children go to lunch just before throwing themselves onto the tracks, or just after having murdered a child and stuffed them under a hotel room bed. The waiters always agree that they had an appetite, that they seemed carefree and polite. We are ninety-nine percent normal, say the parricidal, the difference is only one percent. That's all that separates us from criminals, one percent. A mere before and after, nothingness itself. I think about these deviations that lead nowhere and only take up time as I chew strawberry-flavored gum. I chew one piece after another, corroding my teeth, I blow a bubble, it's the kind they like, I keep buying the whole boxes that are displayed next to the cashiers at the supermarket. Sugar-free, just how J likes them, with a liquid strawberry center, just how E likes them. I stay until Auchan closes, there are fewer options on the weekends and I prowl around other potential places I might spot them. I saw them twice in the alcohol aisle, vodka-based liqueur, rum-based aromatics, aperitifs, pastis digestif, prosecco, cava, semidry champagne, he was filling up the cart, sparkling wine, cider, cocktails, and the children were helping him efficiently, they had formed a chain, their father passed the objects to one of them and then they would pass it on to the next. Like in a war, with volunteers passing food and first aid for the soldiers, afterwards everything will end up in the underground swimming pool that they never declared to the tax authorities. Seems like this big celebration is planned, with couples and friends from the area, with other children their age, and they'll probably all stay the night in the bunk beds, the mezzanines and the attics, the adults passed out, glass in hand, all over the house's spacious floors. Afterwards, a few guests will sell their vineyards, enter into the magnificent downward spiral of debts owed to the public treasury and one day throw themselves off the Saint-Satur viaduct in the early hours of the morning. I walk along the aisles, I know where the security cameras are now, then I spend a long time hidden in the men's bathroom in case one of them runs in to pee, already leaking in their underwear. It's always the same, the pee after a full day at school, although they usually prefer to piss on the classic motorcycles parked outside by the neighborhood fanatics. I make my way towards the toy aisle, I used to be able to steal a battery-powered robot for them, I'd pay for one and hide another in my T-shirt or inside my shorts, that used to make them laugh and laugh, when I finally pulled out the hidden toy once we were sitting in the car, we would feel giddy with the magic of it. Look where mommy found another one, surprise, out it comes from inside my shorts, my underwear, like a rabbit out of a top hat. I saw them twice after the sentence, I'm not sure if they said hello or not, I think they did, one of them with a wave, the other with a smile, me with both a wave and a smile. I walk down the aisles filled with sockets, extension cords, and electric cables, everything is going to come out, it's obvious, total desire, histrionic joy, delirium, it makes me nauseous. Hunched over, I walk towards the parking lot for a round of retching, heaves that increase in intensity, my pelican mouth at full capacity. That's when I see the three of them come out with the crammed shopping cart and open the doors of the new car from a distance, what type of car is that, I never knew anything about cars, an Audi, a Clio, a convertible, an army truck, whatever it is, it's brand new. They both help their father put everything in the trunk, bottles and packaged whipped-cream desserts. I go inside again but the supermarket is closing. Please, please, I jump up and down childishly and do a Latin dance in front of the shutters and they let me in running, sweaty, a ridiculous woman. I buy smoked pork sausages, mustard, vinegar, and bacon-flavored bags of chips, frozen food, bags of Thai rice, and I carry it all in the pouch of my sweatshirt, thank you, thank you, you're very kind. I think they look at me with disgust, they wouldn't touch me even if I gave myself away at the local used car lot. Count me out, I won't be giving myself to anyone, you never know what a person might become.

At the sentencing my government-subsidized housing is deemed too narrow, a corridor with hardly any windows, which traps in the heat. During the sentence my house has fallen into disrepair, not fit to receive the brothers, I can only see them once a month in a supervised place, getting even less than terrorists' families. A neutral place where I can see their father smoking one cigarette after another during our time together. Sometimes I lose track of the conversation and the games we have to play thanks to the smoke their father exhales. Puff, puff, puff, he makes clouds and constructs messages in the air, he's trying to tell me something with those swirls, they distract me, I told him so, but I think the social worker present in the room didn't like what I said, she wrote something down in the report, so I didn't mention it again. For the first few months I wore what I usually do, I didn't dress up, who'd want to wear something gold, with embroidered straps or a pink sweater with appliqué. From the moment I woke up I would wait with a coffee in hand in front of the Loire until it was 3:30 p.m., and then I would walk to the center. I would spy on one house and then the next, all the way along the deserted Saint-Satur, most of the houses were abandoned, I could see the Gothic decor in those enclosed, stifling living rooms, the domes blackened by fires, the long wooden chairs scattered beneath the trees where once their residents must've drank until they passed out. Sometimes, when I had enough time to spare, I would pull off the chains or jump over a gate and sneak inside one of those dumps that two centuries ago were luxurious and majestic and are now only occupied by drunks and addicts, the nocturnal herds in search of their fix. When the state finally assigned me a public defender, she looked me up and down and said: Madame, there are dress codes that you must respect if you want any chance at winning. In cases such as yours, you cannot wear leather, or animal print, or low-cut blouses, or platform heels, it won't help you, do you understand? I cannot represent you if you do not cooperate. That same night she sent a text that I read sitting on the Sancerre roundabout in which she listed out the clothing items I should wear on meeting days, like a type 2 diabetic's diet. The fountain water flowed along the dirty canals packed with fish below my feet, it got dark very quickly that day while I thought about the clothes I had to buy in the Colruyt supermarket or the Gemo discounts, black pants, I don't have any, feminine or plain shoes, I don't have any, a light-colored blouse, no patterns, I've never had any, go to the hairdresser's, I never go. Your image could work in our favor when we appeal the judge's decision, my lawyer says. My image, my tone of voice, my posture. Don't lean so far forwards, don't gesture so wildly with your hands, don't speak with a gruff voice, etc. But progress is made extremely slowly in this country, madame, things change at a snail's pace. In the meantime, don't wear combat boots, don't wear studs, take off any chains, even the delicate ones, fix your hair, work on your softening your expressions and gestures. Number 1: Do not come across as too masculine because you won't seem maternal enough. Number 2: Do not come across as too feminine, to avoid suggesting a pronounced inclination towards sex or obscenity. Number 3: Do not give the impression of being a loner, it looks antisocial, and when the case is heard, they could accuse you of being a social outcast. Try to remain somewhere in the middle, to dress and act in a composed manner. When she saw the photos of my house, it was the same, far too squalid as if you lived in the thirteenth century with crumbling, moldy walls. She made me create a new image for the judges. Paint the walls, move the furniture, find a good angle so there's more light. I did just that, I decorated the house with vases, picked flowers, bought framed pastoral landscapes in the flea market along the Loire. I put a bedroom together for the two of them, no bunk beds yet but good mattresses, the boys like that, jumping from one mattress to the other, their unopened presents on top of the unused bed.

Between each visit, what can be done, madame court-appointed lawyer, waiting for the month to pass, what can be done, my question like a song in a tragic, never-ending scene, like the howl of a dying woman: what, what. Please don't call so often and especially not outside of office hours. What can I do? Do whatever you feel like, but do not approach their residence. How close am I allowed to get, madame? I can't answer your every question, I'm busy in court, I'm in hearings all day, I have other clients, but let's be reasonable, OK? Basically you can't go anywhere near their village, during this period stay at least six miles away, so you can be sure not to make a mistake calculating the distance. Draw an uncrossable line in your mind, an imaginary, six-mile-long line. If you violate this restraining order, it will count against you in terms of revoking your sentence, if your judgment is upheld, madam, well, the court of appeals won't offer any way out of your case. What case? Don't make me explain every single difficulty and juncture with your case, don't make me spend double the necessary energy just on you. For the last time, you're not my only client, I can't represent you if we don't see eye to eye, if we're not on the same side of this fight, which will be long and costly but that we do have a chance at winning one day. Let's be reasonable and let's be patient, alright? Au revoir. Let's be reasonable, I said to myself, crossing the old suspension bridge across the Loire, so beautiful with its hidden corpses that I cried a little. If someone saw me at this moment I'm sure they would think I'm crying because of how miserable I look. To have everything and be miserable, to have nothing and be overjoyed, all the possible spiteful combinations and more. I once got hold of his home telephone number, and I called a few times in the middle of the night and then hung up. In those days, waiting for the monthly visit, what to do, any work at all as long as it's legal, work that would help build up a more solid CV. Have a place to live, car, stable job, payslip, social life, favorable environment, and resources. And so the decorated house, the photos of the boys' bedroom, the new clothes, and the blank contract to work in the vineyards. The whole year, the planting and the harvest. All of it was sent to my assigned lawyer, attached to the email, signed and scanned using the printers in that copy center in town. But, what else? Nothing, madam, the secretary at the family court said, for the last time, we've done everything we can for now, wait, anything else you do from now on would only hurt your chances. I asked in the Psychological and Social Assistance Center in Cosne. There's nothing else you can do, you're on a waiting list, you will receive a hearing date. Could you call the court or the tribunal to ask how long we have to wait for the summons? I can't, the most important thing is that you make sure there are no more reports or evidence filed against you.

The rest of the time you can exercise, do you practice martial arts? My hands sweat, I can't sleep, all I can do is eat until I feel sick and sink into the floor. Go and see a professional, a support group, do some manual work in a team, but I went to those places already, and in the middle of someone else's breakdown I would always stand up, apologize, and leave.

We don't decide anything over the course of a lifetime, we follow our own lives meekly along signposted paths, half-heartedly trying to catch up, teetering on the edge of the abyss, asking the wrong person for help, hitchhiking along a dangerous highway, fleeing when it would've been better to stay, staying by accident. At most we catch up for a few miles, like running a night marathon alongside a cargo train, you can't ask for much more. We don't decide anything about our love lives either, the quickening adrenaline, the red-hot lava. The long marriage, the holiday camp romance, incestuous desires, in an old people's home, an asylum, a palliative care center, in a luxury euthanasia clinic, most use the same words to say the same thing: that you die without the faintest idea. What kind of lives would you like to have lived, gentlemen? No idea. What do you regret, ladies? No idea. We could do it all over again and everything would turn out differently. Born in the same bed, to the same mother, the same day, the same year, a different life. I could've never been born and everything would be the same. The same house next door with its moles and blackcurrants, the same trees cut back and burned in a bonfire at the first sign of winter. Nobody could answer one simple question: why did they choose a life of solitude, or one divorce after another, or a marriage that ends in a race to see whose health will be first to take a nosedive? Once again I think about all this fractured nonsense to pass the time while I lift and entwine the grape vines, straighten the stakes, tighten the wires, and sort the buds. The supervisor, the owner's nephew, oversees all of this work. We jump from one bed to the next, from one chair to the next, in intensive care, in the room where they play cards and everyone just shrugs. In the end amnesia does the dirty work that nobody else wants to do and sweeps everything away. Most die in cloud-cuckoo-land, why did they take the path leading this way instead of the one in the opposite direction, they can remember events, when they deserted the army, when they fell for a minor and would secretly meet her in the barn, but they don't remember why or how, if she had braids, if she had the body of a child, what it was that made them so senile. He continues to supervise me, he watches every move I make as if I were his slave, it's the twenty-first century, Hey, I tell him, it's the twenty-first century. We cross the canal on foot, on a motorcycle, we head towards the cliff or the waterfall, always wandering, but this is as far as I got, thinking too much about this abstract and useless nonsense makes my movements less precise. It's time to clock out. Sorry, all good, see you tomorrow. I can't afford any criticism at work, or to attract any warnings from the boss, it all gets put in my file.

I decide to start riding a bike again, it was on sale, it has several gears and lights for the darkest nights, and sometimes I can see myself head-on, a wild boar with neutral eyes and me in complete darkness. Once, when I had the boys, I took them on a ride, swerving to avoid the owls and the bats, all three of us screaming at the top of our lungs. They asked me in the middle of the countryside if it was true that they swallowed spiders while they were sleeping. They've left school now, I know what they're doing, what they should be doing. I managed to get to this age without an electronic ankle tag, I don't want to end up sitting at some bar in Sancerre telling all the drunks the story of what led me to this debacle, to this shriveled body, something I did one day without even noticing that I cut my life short. I ride my bike over the slippery sand dunes, it's cold now, the crabs and the snails have found shelter. I imagine what they're wearing, their striped sweaters or the ones with the diamond pattern that their grandmother bought them this season, I know how she wraps them up like onions, their puffer jackets that I never wanted her to buy for them. They've left now, they've been sent to wash their hands before eating, they're sitting at the table now, she's made them their poached eggs now, they're watching television in the game room now while their grandfather stirs the embers in the hearth. I look at the plants and the long stems growing beneath the sand. The world is far too vast, the land of aurora borealis, fjords, tundra valleys, salt flats, icebergs, and gulfs, but at the same time, the world is so tiny, so narrow, a blind alley like my rented home, a village with a church and post office. A roundabout for the drunk to walk around, his face bloody. The sun should be coming up by now, surely. I want it to rise, let it rise several times in the same morning, there are still five days to go until our bodies collide. Sometimes I imagine huge things, a scorched city, La Charité-sur-Loire lit up by blazing flashes of light, the grayish match above my children's heads, their hair gray.

It's time, they're dropped off at the school entrance, there's five minutes to go until half past. My lawyer also asked me to be careful with my language in front of the social worker and the employees at the center, ex-offenders in civil rehabilitation. Nobody will notice if I walk past the gate, if I watch as they give their father a kiss, a kiss for their grandmother, as they throw away the pink chewing gum I gave them. Their father doesn't let them chew gum at school, I gave it to them to put in their inside pockets, others give their children fourteen-inch-long kitchen knives. They won't notice if I park over there. My heart races, how clichéd, but I managed to see them go in with their heavy backpacks, I didn't want them to use those so I'd found some with little wheels, but their grandmother insisted, those were the days of the first little bells ringing, the first warnings. I saw them, I saw them, it's the effect on the brain that drives you crazy, how else to put it, a state of bliss, it's the same as when a senile person recognizes their child for just one instant, just a lapse in their dementia. I saw them, my J and my E, I spotted them instantly, in the blink of an eye, before the jailer takes them away, they were with their classmates, I don't know any of their names, but mine were there. Next time I'll climb that tree with the tall branches and then I'll be able to see how they're dressed, what their hair looks like, if their shoes are polished. That day the vineyards seemed steeper and the young supervisor congratulated me on how well I worked: diligent, methodical, energetic. Get back to the house, down a bowl of spaghetti with red sauce and cheese, grab a few half bottles, go to the doorway to watch the dogs that wander around without owners, and occasionally toss them a piece of bread, smoke like my ex-husband smokes, one cigarette after another. But, in the middle of the second drag, I look up at the sky and think about how they're going to sleep soon, brushing their teeth and pretending to count every tooth on the top and the bottom, right now they're switching off the light, I want to see it, why can't I, if I were a gecko under a piece of the furniture I would be able to see them, if I were a rat hidden among vegetables in the storeroom I would see them, why do I see nothing, my ash simply falls between my fingers, just give me a little camera at least, I'm going to ask the lawyer if that's a possibility.

I wake up a long time before the day begins, I dreamed about a creature somewhere between a dog and a fox, I go over the list, the tights, the pointy shoes, the trousers, the colors, not too dull but not too garish, don't give the impression of being an outsider, but don't seem excitable either, not resentful of life, but also not too thrilled to live it. I walk to the place and arrive very early so I don't seem too agitated, so the vein on my forehead doesn't show. My heart takes a while to slow back down after a long uphill walk. I was taught to hold my breath and push it outwards as if I were taking a shit. I fix my hair in the rearview mirror of a souped-up motorcycle and walk into the hall. An assistant greets me and writes down my number and the time on a form. They point me towards a table with three chairs and I wait, my hands resting on my purse. I brought them action figures, gum in various flavors, bookmarks that smell like different fruits and vegetables. The three of them arrive punctually, their hair neatly combed, he always does what he must, never anything against the law, no matter what. Slit a throat, but within the law, call oneself a pacifist while aiming a Kalashnikov, within the law. I asked and they told me it wasn't a good idea, it was better not to cry, not even eyes shiny with tears, but on the other hand I shouldn't laugh either, nothing theatrical, nothing brusque, just be a woman sitting there playing cards, monopoly, doing a hundred-piece puzzle, with that I can get a hearing, right? Didn't you say that this way I can request an appeals court decision in Bourges? He reads his text messages, listens to his voicemail, flicks his lighter on and off, blows out smoke, smiles about something. He has an hour and a half to relax, and I have an hour and a half to be a mother. I can't miss a thing, if I look at the wall or the ceiling, if I get distracted by something about the social worker's face, I feel poisoned, look at your two sons, flowers that grew out of shit, they're right in front of you, right there, a few inches away, now you can touch them, they can kiss you, hello mom, they say. Hello. They say things are good at school, in swim class, with the family. We work on the puzzle with a picture of a boat, which they chose over others with pictures of mountains and castles. I give them their little gifts, we unwrap them over the table and we chew, we blow balloons, they let me touch their hair, tuck it behind their ears, they let me high five them, they let me laugh at how their teeth look like toasters, they let me ask them if they have head lice. I tell them that where I live you can hear owls howl, they don't howl mommy, they hoot, they say, barn owls, snowy owls and other night birds hoot, I hope the social worker noted down that he called me *mommy*. Night birds, I say to them, taking out a chocolate bar even though I know they can't eat it, sounds like they work in the cabaret, and I laugh for a long time, but I quickly recover. I want to see what else I have in my bag, but when I feel the tip of the knife, what if they find it, what if they decide to search me on the way out. I give them some comic books they've already read, they give them back. I ask them how they're doing without me, good, good, I tell them what they were wearing the other day, they don't understand, I tell them that I'd been hanging around nearby. Outside their father flicks his cigarette butt into the flowers and heads towards the entrance, it's time. I can't approach him or make eye contact. I want to say something to them but the social worker takes them and I watch them hurry away.

What am I being accused of? What are the exact words of the accusation? Did you not read it? You should be familiar with every detail. Of domestic violence aggravated by the presence of minors. What type? Punches, kicks, scratches, slaps, assault with flammable material, threats using one or several unidentified sharp objects, aggravated by the presence of the minors in question and multiple witnesses. You are accused of maladaptive behavior, intimidation, and subjecting your spouse to harassment. Madame, let us be clear: in total there are one hundred and fifty letters in support of the allegations against you. Furthermore, there is also the false complaint with the scratches that couldn't be proven. How can I make the situation as clear as possible? It's going to be thorny, there are more than one hundred and fifty testimonies against yours. No, they're not witnesses, they're enemies, they're his allies, in any case, madam, it's shaky ground and it could open up and swallow us, it could swallow you. The plaintiff didn't even want to agree to this physical contact once a month. On the way back, the sand dunes again, the course of the river altered by the cascading night, one night after another night, like a brain hemorrhage, the violent currents, the dazed thoughts like gunshots that fail to go off, fake resistance fighters, informing on collaborators, collaborators passing themselves off as heroes, fake medals for the fallen just before the armistice. A monument with the names of the fallen next to the only bakery where you can find a plum cake. I savor it next to the burned-down church within its wooden shell, it must be about 900 years old. What was it like at dawn on the day of the fire, at what moment did the town's inhabitants wake up to the smell of burning. Had they already bathed, dried their hair, exterminated the lice, what went through their minds before the pogrom reduced everything to ash, they probably fought a few bare-knuckle rounds. Will they occasionally mention me without meaning to, in passing, an unfamiliar name, will they refer to me as their parent? I scarf down the cake, I want to go inside the church but the door is sealed and it's padlocked, I imagine the kneeling faithful in medieval times, the smoking houses all around. I start my rented car for the first time and cross into their area, the glove compartment is loaded, I pass into their territory with its hidden passages and tunnels, their village, with its stables, its go-kart track. It's not yet the thick of night, I accelerate, I've never gotten this close, no need to stop, not now in the middle of a crusade, on the other side of the tunnel, the same side where we used to fight each other surrounded by antisemitic graffiti and phone numbers for in-home sexual services. Under the bridge where he used to scratch me, bite me, where I used to shake him, where we used to assault each other before and after putting the newborns to bed. Right there where the witnesses swear before the law they saw me hit him over and over again on the head and self-flagellate, right there where we kissed and our love was born. Where did his witnesses see us from? Were they hanging over the road? Right over the place where we would fight so the children wouldn't hear us, shhh son of a bitch, shhh motherfucker, where we even threw ourselves down onto the cobblestone path, one atop the other. I slow the car down, it creeps along after I pass through the tunnel until it finally stops. I walk up to the living room windows. Three windows are lit up, voices in the kitchen, coming from their rooms, from the laundry room. The smell of my children, their incipient sweat, the smell of their wet towels, their bedsheets, the smell of their talc, the smell of their bodies in the morning and at night. They can't see me, I can keep moving between the garbage cans and the Chinese privet. A dividing wall separates the house from the canals infested with reptiles and parasites. I crouch in a starting position so I can watch them for as long as possible. They look happy, but we all know what happiness is like. The social worker wrote it in the report on the day of my visit to the home of the main guardian: the children get along well in the absence of their mother. I see the nightlights in my parents-in-law's house. In the garden, the iron reclining chairs that I'd painted, the vegetable garden I planted, destroyed by summer storms, and my underwear hanging next to the black tights, mom's long legs hanging from the wire.

On the way back, the wind blowing against my freezing face, real and fake bruises and scratches on my arms and neck, fake and real police reports with photos, fingerprints, and my personal possessions seized. Everything confiscated, impounded, clothes, documents, my telephone and the sim card with all my contacts in ziplock bags. They can't sleep over in the narrow rented house, more than the agreed-upon thirteen miles away, but less than twenty-five miles away from the minors. I can't sleep either, I get into bed a little drunk, well fed, a few small pre-Christmas discount bottles and all of it absorbed like a hand grenade explosion. I walk back and forth along the corridor of death. Back and forth like white phosphorus. I put my hands over my eyes but I can still see them. I cross the road to the refuge for cripples, workers, and other dregs of society, I sit and drink at the bar, I cross back over the road. I masturbate without taking any pleasure in it, just for the sake of doing something, like spinning the chamber in Russian roulette. The next day I walk around the neighborhood, I see young boys with backpacks larger than their backs, a pair wearing ski hats, which I think is them, I follow them, they turn their heads as they cross, I keep my distance so they don't notice me and get scared. I search for them around the school, another pair looks like them but once I get closer I see their bodies are different, like old children or prisoners. The white sun over the vineyards is a flying saucer. I work for the entire day but badly, lazily. The inspector makes a gesture pulling me aside to speak to him privately, so that the other workers don't notice. I walk down the hill without any idea of what I might say, I'm pale, aged, premature. I just want to take them to see race cars fly from ramp to ramp, drive on two wheels, go off course, drive through a wall of fire and gasoline. The day finishes and I return to the bakery and then to their windows, but now I'm not satisfied with only being a spy, spitting on the informers' houses isn't enough, I want to leave them a message, a map of an island, a motorcycle for when they can come and visit me. Leave them something in the middle of the night like a fan who climbs toward their idol, ready to do whatever it takes, like an incognito semen donor. I fall asleep on the prowl, and when I wake up, the lights are off, the fire is out. The front house too, the broadcast by the intellectuals from the eighties is over and the parents-in-law have passed out. I leave, avoiding the ground wires, and arrive at my car nestled in the forest. I lie down in the back seat. In the center of the night, I am spinning the chamber.

In the following days, I don't go to their windows or to their school, I can't call the court again, they recognize my voice even if I pretend to be someone else. I successfully infiltrate the local pool, the other mothers in headscarves take food wrapped in aluminum foil or cardboard boxes, they pack bags with goggles and swimsuits, shampoo, they wait and chat, sitting on the benches that surround the cold or the heated pools. I buy a blue swimsuit from a vending machine, a swimming cap, I pay the entrance fee of a few euros and go in, entirely law-abiding. I hear voices in the women's changing rooms, I can't hear what they're saying but I imagine myself putting the swimsuit on backwards, throwing everything into the lockers, searching for forgotten coins in the metal lockers. When they line up in a single file and head towards the pools, passing through the showers, I come out of the changing rooms. I don't have visible marks anymore, just some scratches that could be hickeys on my neck and my arms, a few bruises on my calves and buttocks that could've come from dance aerobics, or skating on the national team, or in a hockey championship. I dive into the heated pool. They're here, but my swimming cap and goggles are my disguise, they won't notice me. I manage to swim in the opposite direction and feel the water from their kicking legs, swimming against the current with steady strokes, feeling the water their splashes send my way. When the teacher tells them to get out of the pool, I put my head under the water but I follow them, two wet little ducks in their tricolor swimming trunks. In the winter, the night shows up early like a criminal, I walk using my phone flashlight to guide my path, my hair full of chlorine and my eyes red, I raise a glass to my courage in the bar full of long-distance truckers, driving their gigantic cargo trucks with trailers. How do they manage to drive such monstrosities all the way from Europe to the Middle East? I congratulate you, truckers, I say, and we all drink a toast and then sing in unison in the highway bar. If I were to show them what's inside my glove compartment, they might not be so nice, but I leave it at that. Now hardly anyone notices the marks or scratches. According to the specialized detectives, these marks couldn't have been caused by anyone other than myself. I've never scratched myself, officer, I declared in the police station, unless you did it in your sleep, said a young cadet. DNA never lies, madam, and they carried out a simulation of the scratching on me with a police officer who played his role. I'm tired of getting up at the crack of dawn to go to the vineyard, my bank account is almost empty, the gas tank only has a few liters left, I keep waiting for the next visit but it doesn't come close to satiating me, the drunk who will only accept Spirytus vodka, who rejects anything low-proof and downs bottles of nastiest perfume and cleaning products. Once or twice I climb the tree from which I can see the school fence, the inner courtyard with the Ping-Pong table and the basketball hoop, my children inside, chewing, shrieking with laughter, the other mothers coming and going, their heads held high. The three of them are enclosed by water and salt, by choirs, by dead sea.

And I see us, myself and my husband with our hands around each other's necks, being dragged through the village of the ponds, the neighbors asleep in their bunk beds, the brothers are eyewitnesses.

I sit at a bar, the chairs and cups are covered in spiderwebs, I wonder which men have had their last drink here, I scour my mind for a way to make the flames grow. I terminate the search. One of them is outside dancing on the wooden boards, I can see the other one lying on the sofa with an apple. I take photos, I record videos, they will be useful one day. I call him for the first time, it's not allowed, he tells me, you know this. You have to wait. I see him smoke, I see him surrounded by them, hello. Hello. Hello. You can't call me. I know. So don't call me, be patient and hang up. Don't hang up, but he already has. I call again. I can't hear you properly, but I can. Can I speak to them? You're forcing me to report this. Time will pass quickly. They aren't here now, they went to have dinner at my parents', they asked to go because we're leaving. What do you mean you're leaving? Where are you going? We're going to surf at my friends' place in the south. And he hangs up, caressing one of their heads. The last of the smoke curling up into the air from my cigarette butt crushed into the ground makes me wonder. Wide awake, I lie down behind the sandbanks where the vagrants sleep, where once upon a time there must've been pirates and smugglers. From their loft window my parents-in-law look out at the panoramic view with their eagle eyes, the gate, their bedrooms.

How can I force them out like rats from their hidden den, give them something to make them pass out, make them weak. I walk around the house surrounded by the tall, ancient European horse chestnuts, the frosty wind sweeps up swirls of leaves in huge quantities and scatters them with a musical hum.

In the adjacent farmyard there are large drums, dead leaves, bird shit and stacks of straw. I could easily approach from behind the great-grandmother's deserted house and set fire to the farmyard. The flames would grow around the dry grass with enough fuel to alert the father-in-law and the husband with the sensation of heat. I flick the lighter and bit by bit the mountain of hay lights up, shimmering, gleaming, climbing higher until the entire farmyard is ablaze. It doesn't take long for the devastation to reach the roof. Soon afterwards I see how they smell the stench and go out looking for water and a fire extinguisher. I see them in their dressing gowns and underwear, infuriated. The speed of the fire is more than they can contend with. Something must be done. The mother-in-law comes out of her house, yelling. I walk through the old front gates for the first time since the sentence, go past the shrubs that serve as a dividing wall, the garden. I move through the house like a ghost, I pick up the lightest one and in the confusion of the flames I leave him in the back seat and run to find the second, rescuing bodies from an ambush by fanatics, and I take him and put him on top of his brother. In that instant their bodies don't look recognizable anymore.

Soon the rooster will crow, unless it's been burned to a crisp along with the chickens and the eggs. A few chickens appear, pecking at insects, hunger drives them to eat a large quantity of soil and it makes them sluggish. The rooster deposits sperm in the opening of the chicken's cloaca, if she is fertilized, there will be offspring, if not then fried eggs. The gifts, food, and the tent are already in the back of the car, underneath a burlap sack. The engine sounds like a wagon driven by old horses. I turn against the direction of traffic on the main road, the chickens come out of a neighboring structure and walk along the road like dazed survivors. The village's chimneys expel impure soot, powdery, they need a chimney sweep but the local one retired. I turn at the public basins where if I'd been born in the autumn of 1877 I would be plunging underwear and blankets into the water, and I would have the right to a domestic life, short, flat. I keep going past the two-story house with a veranda, we're in the late 1920s, a couple met within those walls just before the offensive. After vacations in the Alps and climbing mountains together as lovers, they now both have dementia and live together as perfect strangers. They pass one other in the bathroom in the middle of the night and start shouting: Help! Help! They pass one other in the hallway where their fiftieth wedding anniversary paintings hang and they call the gendarmerie to report a break-in. The neighbors take them bread and cider at Christmas and every time they introduce them anew: lovely to meet you, says Lucette, lovely to meet you, says Bernard, and they fall in love. Love is born, love dies, love is born, love dies, it connects and disconnects so many times in one lifetime, like an electricity grid. I've nearly reached the end of the village, I circle a marshy pond with water spiders and an alligator, jumping around it are two carnivorous Rottweilers.

I still can't believe what I've just done, I still can't believe I'm not in that narrow house, fantasizing. The wind flattens the malnourished foals, the electric fences, and the young hedgehogs. The snow could melt or it could become a lethal weapon. Before everything started, that last night we told one another that someone was going to get hurt. He announced that he was going to protect himself and make sure his rights were respected. How? I asked him, are you going to buy an air gun? I will defend myself, you'll soon understand the legitimate right to self-defense and the principle of innocent until proven guilty. Ah, the great refuge of the guilty. Neither of us studied law, it doesn't matter, we'll speak like them, one day we'll set up an office together. Here I come, a mother behind the wheel just like the others with their headscarves and packed lunches, just like the ones who walk into the school, then come out, their heads held high as they walk past the gendarme. It's getting light, on one of the last nights the children climbed into our bed, I felt them moving from their mattresses like immigrants on their inflatable rafts. They are sunk, they deflate, nobody learned how to swim, one moment of panic and everyone falls into the water like dominoes. If I was drowning with two hundred migrants above me I would crush whoever was necessary in order to breathe, if I was entrenched within a human mountain and I heard the fanatics coming, I would hide underneath other bodies. I look through the rearview mirror and they are still asleep.

I drive with my eyes fixed on every passing stretch of the pavement. I drive without taking my eyes off the white lines on the road. One, two, three, infinite white lines taking us further and further away. I don't care about anything else, I have them, when they wake up we can celebrate the prison break, the reunion, the successful hostage exchange, we can stop for breakfast, decide together what to do next. When they find me, if they find me, I'll bring them back along the route following the iron aqueduct over the canal, its barracks converted into asylums. They will have freshly laid eggs for dinner, the yolk hard with sperm cells, they will talk about the burned-down house, about the insurance, the rebuilding, the repairs, the incinerated wooden trough as a souvenir of the crime, the final judgment. She showed us who she really was in no time at all. Silence! The grandparents will shout at them with a hard smack, no talking at the table, and they will all eat, noisily chewing their mouthfuls of baguette. The French language is the language of order, Spanish, the great disappointment. Time to sleep! My in-laws will say, no arguments. It must be around six in the morning, or a little earlier, people around here leave the shutters closed until further notice. The car rattles and uses up more gas. The road signs warn of potentially lethal accidents due to drivers falling asleep. There's nobody on the A77, during a long stretch past the A26, A27, A28, A29, A30 exits, I don't see a single other vehicle, just a school bus on the shoulder but not a single cargo truck carrying weapons to Bakhmut. When I get to the A32 exit I take the downhill road towards the entrance of the village Pougues-les-Eaux, I'm twenty-five miles from the house and no one noticed, the chimney smoke is still peacefully billowing into the air in dense, low clouds, like a friendly poisonous mushroom. I stop in the Pouilly station, the ditches are filled with the metal skeletons of burned-out, abandoned cars. I look both ways before getting out. Standing in front of the gas pump, I struggle to fit the hose into the opening of the tank.

I have them with me, here they are, I feel euphoric, I'm out of control, that's euphoria, isn't it? How could anything be under control, I have them with me, I look at them, I shut the car door, I open it. I see how every now and then they twist their necks and slide down in their seats. I'm so hungry, I start eating behind the wheel, the food falls down between my legs, when I had them we always used to vacuum the seats together, we would clear out the cookies, the candy, we would find hidden treasures, hoops, toys, coins. The boys will be in my arms, as long as eels, unless they don't want this, unless they reject their savior. What would the lawyer say, she would quit, she would sue me, she would sell me to the opposing team, what would the public defender's assistant say? I still don't have any messages or missed calls, it hasn't been more than an hour, my parents-in-law must be enveloped in flames.

We have traveled far enough now to stop and pee. I wonder when they'll sound the alarm throughout the entire county, if they won't go and look for them in the village first, including the water tanks, dragging everyone along on a candlelight vigil, if they don't try negotiating with a tapped phone line first. If they don't go and search for them in the charred rubble first, I wonder if they'll leave flowers and teddy bears. I get out of the car to smoke, I watch J and E, and remember the moment we chose their names. I see them through the blurry window, they're sleeping, but suddenly, my smile vanishes, I realize that their eyelids are twitching and they might just be pretending to be asleep, they're pretending so they can open the door and jump out, run across the fields screaming for help. A farmer finds them or they find a public telephone, they go into an old lady's house and beg her to find their father. I see myself in the reflection, my feeling of calm disappears, I feel the suspicion of a pig just as it realizes it's going to be slaughtered and chopped up, just not yet. They both love pigs, going to the farm, petting them, swallowing them. I assume they don't understand that it's the same animal, the one that lies in the sun and the one they swallow, this nonsense in my head, once again I'm in the mental swamp. When they wake up, what will they say, what will they see in me, once they finally wake up, what will they want to do, hang a sign around their necks, run along the highway making hand signals, celebrate by jumping up and down on a triple motel bed.

The rooftops, the deserted churches, everything covered by that first purifying snowfall. The snow scrubs away the fleas, the stench, the dead ferrets slung onto the sidewalk. What is he doing now, rushing around the house with his hands clutching at his neck, on foot, mortifying his flesh with iron nails, the soles of his feet twitching, searching for them like a wild bull, sounding the alarm at the police station, calling all the neighbors to ask them to make another statement. Yesterday my husband was eating out of my hand, he was throwing the basketball through the hoop, darts into the dartboard, and now life has done a one-eighty. Neither he nor his parents can find them anywhere, *hein*, neither he nor his parents know where they are, *hein*, they suspect, but they don't want to say it, by now they can hear the shrill sound of the worst possible option. But before succumbing to general panic they inspect all the houses in the village, the sheds full of feathers, the lofts with wall-to-wall carpets stocked with liquor and the wine cellars, they go door-to-door.

I sit on the bed, hundreds of flies buzz around the windows, stuck within the folds of the curtains. The walls, the legs of the recently painted pieces of furniture, everything hums as if heard from the inside of an egg. On the floor, a black layer of writhing flies, in the process of dying. Trapped inside the new sheets of the new house, the flies move but cannot fly. I move through the house, looking through the window I notice that my father-in-law didn't switch off the light in the loft where he works. I call to him. He comes in stealthily, on tiptoes and wearing socks, his mouth a cloud of smoke, a dirty cap on his skull. I show him the mess, he puts his hand over my mouth, how disgusting, it's so that flies can't get in. He comes back with a fumigator and pesticide, mask and suit. He hands me an electric racket. I wait for them to get tired, when they land on the racket, I watch them burn, some have far too much of a will to live. Now go and look for the females' eggs, he tells me, they're in the trash. I find the eggs, I line them up, I burn them. I see him take pleasure in killing, poisoning, and taking out a bag full of them. On the window sills and in the sheds, inside sandals and rubber shoes, the remains. How did they get in, we made sure to shut everything, I tell him. They didn't come in, he says, they were already inside, waiting for you.

The world is arid and white. Now the telephone rings, it stops, it rings again. The missed calls pile up. Everything accelerates like an Eastern advance, like the second aerial attack after blitzkrieg. I could have put dolls in the rocking chairs, it would have worked for a while, I could have left a threatening poster, set a homemade time bomb. I could have hired a contract killer for a reasonable amount of money, I could have tied them up, tied them to the legs of the table, a pogrom. I ask myself what I can tell him, if I have to answer, if I should do as he does and leave him hanging. The telephone falls from my hand, and I see how their eyelids flutter. I'll figure out what to do afterwards, who I can ask for help, whether or not to break the phone apart like those missing girls' angel-faced boyfriends. The police will find it later in a hole in the wall. I have to take this one day at a time, and once I'm surrounded, it will be hour by hour, and then it will be settled minute by minute. It rings, I hit the brakes, I jump out of my seat, and answer the call while standing on the shoulder. He's scared. Are they with you? I can hear my parents-in-law talking in the background, they thought the worst of it was behind them and they were starting to talk about remodeling the garages and renting them out to Parisians. I told him in a dry tone, the same he used with me yesterday, that he needed to calm down or I would hang up.

Hello, hello, children, they rub their eyes, hello, it's me, mom, you're going to be with me for a little while, the boys in their puffy jackets, they don't look at one another. Don't worry, your dad stayed behind with your grandparents because a part of the house burned down and I came to rescue you and take you on an adventure. I arrived in the middle of the night to save you from the terrible smoke, I had a dream about you and so I decided to come and see you, I arrived just in time. Don't worry. We'll go back soon, this is just a vacation. Are you hungry?

A police siren wails somewhere in the distance. I turn off the road leading to an expressway. Midday slowly approaches, the boys look out the window, every now and then our eyes meet like blazing lightning. We stop by a grove, a wooden table, and some bathrooms for travelers, we sit down, I take out some bags, now I'm one of those mothers with bags, cheap cookies, potato chips, a soft drink. They need fattening up so they can hibernate, they need reserves, they need to be able to endure long days of fasting if they decide to escape, in case some degenerate mechanic invites them in to see his amazing car. There are kidnap victims who survived sixty days without food, why not them. I still have to figure out where to go, everything leaves behind evidence, on the one hand, we have to think about erasing, concealing, and smudging fingerprints, saliva, secretions, but on the other hand, it's better to show oneself, leave traces, signs that we were alive, wave to the camera, hello, let them see me taking money out of every ATM, let them see me in the seaside bungalow, let them identify me passing through the highway tollbooths. I take the gifts out of the trunk, I tell them to turn around. One, two, three, they open their eyes, they're camouflage suits for the wilderness, is this what you wanted? They put them on and go play among the trees.

Life takes a long time to become real, sometimes it never does. The trouble is that everything ends up being smaller than we thought, I think once we're in the car: we fantasize about the arrival of the moment when life finally makes its entrance, I was able to find my prey hidden behind a couple of tree trunks. We fantasize about life arriving one day, glorious, sensational, we convince ourselves it will explode into being from one moment to the next, but we never know when, we wait eagerly, and in the end, none of it is true. I put on "Don't Dream It's Over," behind us the cows are lying down with their calves, flocks of birds head south, a few fly north to procreate and fill their nests. Hey now, hey now. Don't dream it's over, Hey now, hey now, When the world comes in, this song takes me to the pink, fiery warmth of childhood, to the rash-covered body, to the washed body devoid of libido throughout those snake-filled summers. The whole drive I have this vague sensation of the beach, of summer, of burning sand, the coast with grandparents, uncles, cousins, and camp neighbors, all of them have succumbed, the sensation of the rough sea that could easily drag you out with its little black triangle flag, the throbbing ocean, the sun's citrus scent, digging holes in the sand along the shore. The angst of those days on the coast with the open window facing the empty lot, of retarded children hidden behind the green canvas, of living parents, of unborn children. I used to pull my bathing suit to one side, sitting on the rocks, and imagine that I had to give birth to babies but I didn't know where they would come out. That era of crimes not committed against spouses who serve one other mate and eat pastries kept in Tupperware. The children hug one another until their bones hurt, those siblings love each other to death. They look at me coldly; the reunion between Svetlana Alliluyeva with Chrese Evans, Joseph Alliluyev, and Yekaterina Zhdanova. They go where I take them, they're at my mercy, as they should be. The boys in the back like perfectly trained dogs, like the child Mozart, repeat, repeat. My lawyer will call me any minute, make a huge fuss, and tell me to turn myself in. The magnetism of love, the moment you have someone at your mercy, like in an operating theater with their flesh marked in red, their genitals exposed, the body entirely ready for an incision, a graft, an ablation. Boys, I say, and I turn my head, boys, we're alone now, you're not scared, are you?

A wooden sign announces our entrance to Prémery. A flood of messages just before we're swallowed up by the forest: Can you tell me how they are? Where can I come and get them? When fear defects to the other side, that's the only true justice. No hearing in sight, no judicial response, no strategy, no confrontation. The instant when everything tilts, where can I come and pick them up? Tell me before I call the police. I'm driving very fast, and because I want to read his messages the car is suddenly tilting on two wheels, I turn it into a joke, it's no big deal, just a bump! We're alive! Mom is a great driver, can you tell? The boys hold onto one another. They will inherit euphoria through their maternal line, my legacy. As we enter the forest I lose signal, I'm relieved to no longer receive his pleas, we stop, they piss against a fungus-eaten, sprouting log. Shall we put our suits on again? The three of us undress in the cold, our three butts exposed like easy prey, then we gradually turn into foliage and hide. Afterwards we throw ourselves into the leaves, we roll around, a hunting party scares us. All this time we were apart felt as endless as trench warfare, but it's over now, are you alright without me? They don't know what to say, they play dumb, they play sick. Everything they've told you about mom is a lie. I never did anything wrong. We drive through the forest with the windows up and the doors shut, we cross the whole of Prémery like the waters of Lake Piru. If I die, a sheriff will come and search for my body, he'll bring a tow truck, but first a stalker will see the dirty brothers, ask about their father. As I leave Prémery my phone rings constantly like a heart monitor alarm. Where are they, where did you take them, where have you hidden them. You're going to lose what little you had. He says he went to the hospital in Nevers just in case a neighbor had rushed them there during the fire. They told him that no child with our sons' names had been admitted. He asked them to check again, he snatched from the employee's hand the list of names of children in the waiting room, hospitalized, discharged, and when he couldn't find his children's names, he cursed and kicked the door. He ran through the halls with their coffee machines that spit out filthy concoctions, where parents who would lose their just-resuscitated children that very night are now eating instant soup. He banged on the glass in front of a security guard who asked him to calm down or he would give him a citation for disturbing the peace in a public place.

We travel a hundred and twenty miles without any of us opening our mouths, so much silence that when I ask them if they would like to stop and eat, my voice sounds strange to us and the words start tumbling out. It's nearly dark, incredible, boys, it's nighttime already, I'm astonished; don't we have school, mom? Look at the beetles falling. Look at the beetles, they're like missiles! I park in a camping area with space for tents and wooden cabins on stilts. Everything is very rustic, looking up the hill it's impossible to tell if the cabin has collapsed or is just disappearing into the gloom. I get them out of the car as if I am releasing mountain goats or garden frogs into the wild. They hop around while I look for somewhere to pay to stay the night. I take a few steps, there's a sign boasting about the quality of the old-growth trees, the chestnuts, banana trees, capable of holding out for up to five hundred years. I take the bag with the tent poles, the ropes, the clips, and the rain fly from out of the trunk. J and E walk around, tent stakes in their hands. I stick some into the ground but they're twisted, and suddenly I see a man inside one of the cabins. Romain, he introduces himself, do you need help? The three of us watch how he pulls out the tent stakes and drives them back in in the opposite direction, and then all of us help attach the ropes. We bundle up and put on our ski masks and walk around the edge of the lake. The tent flaps like a boat that's been anchored for decades. Who was that man? No idea, I tell them. We walk back. How lovely to see them eating nuts, tossing tomatoes at one another, blurring into one another, how lovely to see them fattening up, wolfing it down, making their bodies strong. I eat with my hands, without chewing. We could have one another for lunch, if it came to that, it's an acceptable way of life, communal and even moral, to die inside one another. I tell them a story about starving grizzly bears and how they gobble up campers who don't have bear spray or shotguns in Alaska's rocky terrain. I tell them the last words of those men, which were: I don't want to die. Watching them fall asleep is like waiting for the final notes of a melody.

ARMAND: What did your lawyer have to say about this?

LISA: I haven't spoken to her.

A: The fire is attempted aggravated homicide.

L: At a certain point there are no other options ...

A: Are the court-appointed lawyers no good?

L: At a certain point, you do something.

A (*the mother-in-law's voice can be heard in the background*): She's going to pay ...

L: Tell her that I heard her.

A: She says she heard you, she says she doesn't care.

L: The same thing is going to happen to you.

A: So then, you already know what's going to happen to you.

I hang up and it's like everything flies into the air, palm trees, fecund nests, our half-built house, the rabbit holes. The silence around us was absolute, I couldn't hear a single twig crack, not even gusts of wind against the tent. I stand still within the crevice thinking about digging a tunnel, a long tunnel, carrying tons of dirt in bags on my back for the next few years, the three of us digging, like somebody who went crazy over gold and digs underneath their own house, under the neighbors' houses, convinced there's treasure. We eat the sand so that nobody suspects anything, we build the central joists with surimi sticks and bones, we endure the electric shocks from the water when it floods and the electrical connections of the pumps. Afterwards we build new tunnels with blisters on our hands, we smack the backs of our heads against the wooden beams. Everything will be worth it and afterwards we can swim along the river or fly in hot air balloons. A whole life millimetrically designed to leave it behind.

A: Everything was destroyed.

L: The wind.

A: What the judge said.

L: I have them, I'll bring them back to you afterwards.

A (*the mother-in-law's voice*): Attempted murder.

L: Everything burns so quickly with the wind.

A: The authorities have been notified, there's not much more to say.

L: That first time under the bridge, we were happy.

A: Come back Lisa, there's nowhere for you to go.

I listen to the argument between the son and his parents. I see a light approaching the tent like a flying saucer. I get to the tent, the light moves as I unzip the opening and I find them asleep. I don't know the exact date they were born, what day it was, what season it was, if it rained that day, I wish they could never grow up.

A: Your lawyer told us she can't get hold of you.

L: I'm going to explain everything to her and she'll understand, she's a woman.

A: It's in your best interests to ...

L: Give me some time.

A: It's obvious you don't understand the law. I'm passing you to my mother, she wants to say something.

L: I don't want to listen to her.

MOTHER-IN-LAW: People keep coming by the house to show solidarity, to provide testimony. (*To the son*) Can you tell this woman to shut up?

A (*taking the phone away from the mother*): Get out, mom, I'll take care of this.

FATHER-IN-LAW: Becoming a mother, just to go and do this ...

MOTHER-IN-LAW: How much money does she want?

A: Come on Lisa, turn back.

FATHER-IN-LAW (*taking the phone from the son*): Is this about the papers?

A (*taking the phone from the father*): We haven't slept at all.

FATHER-IN-LAW: You're not allowed to drive my car.

A: It's my car.

FATHER-IN-LAW: I paid for it.

PARENTS-IN-LAW: You left it all bloody.

A: We went to the police.

L: But you and I know it isn't true, that we were laughing, that you were happy.

MOTHER-IN-LAW: Tell your woman to shut up.

A bat hangs from a branch and falls asleep.

We open the tent, smile at the water, sweep black flies into little piles with our naked feet, some stick between our toes. We make a pile and throw them into the water. We see them sailing along, face down, some of them already sinking to the bottom, a couple of them bobbing up and down in the ripples like barges. We lie down to eat the last of the sardines and raisins. We lick our lips, we are quickly getting fatter, but what else can we do, how else can we celebrate. Behind us are moles and porcupines as hungry as we are, jumping around. I can feel the vibrations of their paws hitting the ground, I'm suspicious of wild beavers. J proposes we adopt a porcupine for the rest of our adventure, but I'd prefer a squirrel as my copilot, E wants a guinea pig. We play a game, we'll jump on the first animal to cross our path, whoever manages to catch a paw can choose. I suggest we find a net, the two of them search the area. I see a man in the distance walking in my direction but looking the other way. As he gets closer the brothers search for wires, anything to build the trap with. He introduces himself as the property manager, a set of jailer's keys hangs from his belt. I didn't know this land had an owner, I say to him; he has the look of a lifetime employee, it belongs to the municipality madame, but I oversee it. Do I owe you something for the night? We must register your presence and that of the minors. They're on vacation, it's a holiday where they're from. In any case, we still need to make an entry in the register. I understand, you need documents, we'll get our things together and come. Sure, he says, I have a small office in the front cabin. The man walks away, his keys jangling like a carillon hanging from the soft, twistable neck of a bovine. I gather our clothes inside the tent and break it down like a Senegalese street vendor when they hear someone shout the word police in front of the Eiffel Tower. They've already dug a hole, they just have to wait for the rodent to come and then snare it in their arms like scissors. I drive in a curve around the property, making it look like I'm heading towards the office. The man raises his arm, signaling for me to stop, he smiles at me, I accelerate on the grassy ground, I cut across and drive past the cabin at full speed.

We listen to the never-ending story, aaa aaa aaa, never-ending story towards the northeast. I shift gears clumsily, the boys laugh about how I drive. A nocturnal bird of prey, look, it's an anomaly of nature, they should move around at night, glide close to the ground and smell everything that moves, they aren't in their habitat now. It's missing a wing, mom, one of its wings is hanging from its body, did they shoot it? Why would they shoot it? It's a bad omen, a harpy. What do those animals eat? Is it going to attack us? Flesh and carcasses. If we get close will it attack us? I like to watch them jump out the windows as if they were leaping into a water slide. We watch how it spreads its wing and then it lands at our feet. The owl shakes itself off, then takes off and flies around above our heads, suddenly it swoops down low searching for rodents and vermin, it unfurls its wings completely and, ohhh, it's so much bigger, it's a peacock, an eagle! E is frightened, the owl hisses, snaps its beak and begins to move its head aggressively, its heavy head and beak dropping. We get back inside the car, we shouldn't have stopped, I said, I wasn't thinking. Not-think-ing mom, not-think-ing mom!, they sing, but that's not my name you know, I tell them. Did you know that when I was born I wasn't called mom? It's not like I've been mom ever since I was born. So what's your name? Do you have another name? I'm not going to tell you yet, but we can all choose new names for this trip. They can't believe I was born a different person. For the rest of the drive we think of new names for each of us, Johnny, Clarence, Stalina, Billie, Claus, Lev, Lje, X.

I park on an access road, the most important thing is that it doesn't seem dangerous. We aren't safe yet, a rehab-center escapee could appear at any moment holding a wrench, especially here where psychiatric hospitals are hidden behind foliage and where hate for hate reigns, hate for hate and shut up and let yourself be decapitated. I switch off the engine. What a noisy engine, finally we can hear the squalls, the beginning of the tornado. I go out into the cold, I unbutton their jackets, they've peed themselves, they still can't hold it in a moving car, I search for their underwear with ninjas or astronauts. Sometimes I put them on wrong, with the flap in the back, I probably haven't changed their underwear even ten times since they stopped using diapers, and it's always the same thing with me putting them on backwards, stop, you do it wrong, and other hands take care of peeling off their yellow layer. They are so sweet, one passes clothes to the other, one body stretches along the ancient path that the other breaks for them. I put the urine-soaked clothing in a bag and stick it in the trunk, tomorrow we'll find a place for a haircut. I imagine someone who winds up facing a firing squad, standing in front of a line of gendarmes with guns. It's the final hour, you must write a will, imagine your mother's face when she receives the news of your execution, the words, three or four, announcing your dissolution. That's it, you dissipated, you evaporated, you are not here, you are no longer, you never were, you were never born. But no one can even hear your goodbye, goodbye. Just before being led to the wall, they take him to his cell. I imagine that state of neuronal turmoil, of warped signals, of loss of seasonal space. I imagine a cell with forty old prisoners all damned in the halls of death, I imagine a telephone smuggled in secretly, those calls to the outside world, reaching for last-minute salvation, the voices of those who live in the sun. They are going to execute all of us, all of us!, they say, their faces obscured by hoods, from the rooftop of the prison. I imagine the release day of detainee after a Russian sentence, sixty years in a hole, a last-minute stay of execution. The man walks step by step along the path that borders the wall of the prison with a feeling of otherworldly euphoria. Like a lab chimpanzee bred for experiments when it sees the sky for the first time.

The windows steam up with their sleepy breath, it looks like a car that's been sealed shut. I close my eyes and I can see the fire again. How high did the flames climb, could they have reached the clouds? I roll my first cigarette of the day sitting on the hood, thinking about how to steal food from the suburban supermarkets. In the distance, the highway with its trucks and Eastern merchandise, they skip all the checkpoints on their way to the war. Behind, dense white forests filled with needles, blankets donated by the International Committee of the fanatical Red Cross. I've always been drawn to people with no health insurance, who drive stolen cars or buy them on the black market in gypsy camps, who don't pay their rent, who scratch their names from the mailbox, who burn cables and pastures, who drive along the narrow country lanes at three in the morning and steal from the self-service pizza machines. They live a life between walls, fenced-in fields, coming out like raccoons once all of the edges are softened and nothing shines. We have crossed half the country already and yet we are still within their reach, in their gaze, the incestuous, I mean affectionate grandparents, and the handsy neighbors. I look for the phone in the glove compartment, all the missed calls.

A: Where did you take them after snatching them in the middle of the night?

L: We just drove around. Next time we stop, I'm going to throw the phone out of the window.

A: We can still negotiate.

L: What?

A: I can cancel my report and your deportation.

L: Yesterday you said everything was already decided.

A: They need to come home.

L: Yesterday you said it was too late.

A: You're making this worse.

L: All we're doing is going for a ride.

A: Come back before they catch you and take you away like a most-wanted fugitive.

L: If I come back, can they sleep with me a few nights a week and will you give me a divorce?

A: Don't make me laugh.

L: We always used to laugh together. We used to be happy, even when we were unhappy.

A: I'm not sure we were happy.

L: I think we were.

A: The entire village has come together with posters, flowers, teddy bears.

L: Ahh, the teddy bears!

A: You took something that doesn't belong to you.

L: I think you're saying this just to keep me talking so they can track my location.

A: There's also the arson charge. The whole village is in shock, more and more of our neighbor's chickens and rabbits are dying.

L: Is it because of the poison? I've always been afraid of poison, after we moved to the countryside I always checked the bottom of drinking glasses and used my own cutlery.

A: The neighbors are at the door, the mayor came, he's not going anywhere, despite the swastikas.

L: The swastikas! On shed after shed, fence after fence, but the mayor said that a swastika isn't necessarily bigoted.

A: I don't get involved in politics, Lisa.

L: And they didn't get rid of them all, they stopped covering them up because they ran out of white paint.

A: What did they tell you to say?
L: Nothing.
A: Nobody put anything in your drink. You're the poison.
L: Good idea.

I fling the phone to the floor, he hears a fall, my white Dacia Logan falling over a precipice and then muffled turbulence. The three of us in the car, fifty meters beneath dark seaweed.

The table was set for uncles and cousins. Every last detail considered, even the moths in the flowerbeds. We were in the front house, having a difficult morning. The parents-in-law called us the first time, asking us to help them carry firewood, decorate, heat up the unused rooms, the bedrooms with faded upholstery as cold as refrigerators. But we were in bed, everything had started with a gentle joke, a stone rolling down the Alps, a stupid joke about the Jewish moles on my chest and back, a joke that went too far, to the point of not being able to get out from under the blankets. My parents-in-law call their son once at ten o'clock in the morning, twice at 10:15, a third time at 11 and that's the limit, the line you cannot cross when there are guests. My father-in-law with his glued-in dentures and shabby clothes is heading our way. He doesn't have keys but gets in somehow, through some hole, burrowing like a rodent. We heard him on the lawn with his boots up to his knees and we watch as he peeks into every window. We always forget to close them at night, we pull the covers up over our eyes. Son! Are you here? He shouts, wandering around the outside the house, and then from the garden, are you alright? Have they done something to you? We were ashamed, two pubescent kids caught naked in the laundry room. We could sense the father-in-law getting closer, he wasn't turning back, moving through the weeds, crouching, on all fours. The father-in-law is looking for a six-foot ladder, he flicks away his menthol cigarette, we hear him collapse and fall down the chimney. We hear a bang inside the vent and he falls through the tube covered in soot. He's an eccentric, the son says, mother is right about him not being able to live outside an institution. He's been trying to throw himself off a ladder since we moved here and he set everything up for us, the cables, gas, light switches, the dryer, the dishwasher, the water tank, the septic tank and this time he actually did it, it really is just like mother says. We cover ourselves up, go to the living room and find him on the floor, a black, greasy substance covering his face and glasses like an artilleryman. The son gives him a few slaps and he reacts, his glasses askew. Why didn't you answer me, son? Your mother is on the edge of a nervous breakdown, your mother said she needs you by her side. We help him to his feet. I was the one who disinfected his wounds while the son went to collect firewood and calmed the mother down.

The boys look up and laugh. *Coucou*, I hide, they see me and laugh. The law is wrong, if a baby is on the outside during an attack, it's homicide, if the baby is on the inside, as a fetus, there's nobody to blame. If its heart beats even once outside the body, it's murdering a person, but if it was born dead, then there was no murder, clean as a whistle, the executioner can go home or to a reeducation camp. I take the highway towards the northeast. The whole way there's the same yellow sign: DANGER — DON'T FALL ASLEEP. We recommend you install the antidrowsiness device that monitors your heartbeat: at the first sign, it vibrates, the second, the alarm goes off and gets louder. The village is behind us, on a miniature scale. A nineteenth-century village for the chronically insane where they did experiments that they didn't dare to try in Paris. A large psychiatric ward with beds, farms, alfalfa, and chicken coops. The disturbed graze, gather nuts, and look up at the stars. It's going to be a long night, I have to keep my eyes wide open so I don't nod off, fix my gaze on a particular point along the night tunnel and keep moving towards Finistère. Seaside towns are more antisocial, more hesitant to change, there's less gossip. Nobody can say, not even the local authorities, or the neighbors with their houses they passed down for several generations, what goes on inside the fortresses facing the breakwater. Everything takes place with the strictest discretion when the sea levels rise, hangings, stranglings, etc. I drive in silence, signs with blinking arrows shimmer on one side and indicate that we must merge to the right. I slow down as I pass, a police officer waves me through, he looks at my license plates as though he was going to make a note: CW339TX. I'm driving a white Dacia Logan, an adult woman, with her sleeping twins, I don't see what could possibly raise any suspicion. I don't know why I'm so nervous, I could open the trunk for them, turn on the lights in the back, show them what's in the glove compartment, I would even let those drug-sniffing Belgian shepherds in. There are no speed cameras, at the roundabout I take the first exit and continue along the D26 and the Grande Rue, I pass through a construction zone. The first circuit of stage one is complete. It must seem like I'm lurching along, without any sense of direction, Auzits to the Monts d'Aubrac, passing through Salles-la-Source, Sébazac, and Bozouls before descending into Vallon. This isn't going to just stop, I told him so, so many times. Not even with more children or if we escaped together? And we'd return to the tunnel, our underground love, to the scenes that we kept reliving for hours. What did we say to each other? I can't remember, insults and threats on a loop. I want us to have a joint savings account for our old age and retirement and one for the twins, five euros a day is enough so that when they're twenty they can rent an apartment in the suburbs. This isn't going to last much longer, not at all, this blanket of denial. Life doesn't offer even the smallest hint. You rewind the tape with people on a bus, people going to bed on a Friday afternoon, one breath before the carnage and you can't see anything, and just a few hours afterwards, the children's beds are covered in blood. Life is a flat field, there are no pythons, no grenades, no sky with its lightning, just corn and wheat, I park in an orange emergency 112 call point.

A: Lisa, there's nobody we can compare ourselves to, we aren't like anybody else, I'm serious, even in the tunnel we were a little bit happy.

L: We are the incomparables!

A: But to become a mother and then do this.

L: And you became a father and then did this.

A: To get married for this, I never expected it.

L: I didn't expect to see you turn into this either.

A: I didn't turn into anything, I'm the same person I've always been.

L: It's like a religious conversion, suddenly you belong to God.

A: Kidnapping, homicide attempt, a background of domestic violence.

L: You did something much worse.

A: Why do you hate me?

L: Because I made them, it's easy.

A: And you lost them. You know that even though you have them now, they aren't yours.

L: During my LH peaks, you should've run away instead of hiding to play.

A: You know I have a hard time making up my mind.

L: You wouldn't even move, you did it on purpose, you'd be inside me, not moving at all.

A: I always tried do what you asked me to, in fact, I did ejaculate.

L: But you didn't want them, I was the only one who wanted to have them, I remember you saying that you didn't want them, that it was twice the burden, like smuggling capsules of cocaine inside your belly.

A: Don't hang up.

L: Why are you trying to take them from me now?

A: Come back and we can leave.

L: Grant me a divorce and we can share them.

A: I can go.

L: I'm going to file a report on you too, I have a list of crimes with no final judgment.

A: Do you think I feel proud of myself? Do you think I enjoyed doing that to the mother of my children?

The three of us didn't say that he had thrown himself down that hole, just that he had slipped at the top of the ladder, so that the mother-in-law wouldn't start on him. Nobody believed us, but that's what lying is, it doesn't have to seem real, it's about never telling the truth. We ate oily cheeses covered in mold and a rabbit that had gotten trapped in the fence. The night before the visitors I'd stayed up late and I saw a group of brownish-yellow hares right in front of me. I saw the muscles of their extended legs and the father-in-law was like a greyhound, a barrier. What were you doing yesterday in our vegetable garden in the middle of the night? It wasn't me, he said. But we saw you, father. I thought the barnyard was on fire and I went to put out the flames. He started running and stomping on them, he slipped but he managed to catch the fattest one. He hung her from a harness, he let her blood run out, cut off her tail, her ears, and gave it to the mother-in-law as a surprise gift. She woke up, saw it stretched out on her pillow and she stroked it. The hare was prepared with sauce chasseur, carrots, parsley, and bay leaves.

Everything people say about love is wrong. Everything people understand or say they understand is wrong. Love is compensation, it's vengeance. Love is hundreds of aggressive monkeys looting and pillaging believers at the entrance to a Buddhist temple. Any mother whose children's hands are cut off or taken to the other side of the wall would have done this or worse. I don't say mother because I think it's somehow proof of love. The law doesn't understand, the judges don't understand, or they're pretending to be dumb. Rape is permitted as a variation of insatiable love but to kidnap your loved one isn't? Incest is permitted as a last resort but trafficking isn't? It's not acceptable to take justice into your own hands, but stealing babies is? Any honorable person should be in prison. A child is not just a being that came out of another being, we can have a lot of things inside of us, in Mississippi they stick pig organs into gazelles. Like those stories that seem too outrageous to possibly be true, we were returning from a dream journey. What exactly don't they understand? Why are they so shocked? What's so surprising about the billions of possible neuronal connections? Isn't it logical that one would tell you to burn babies alive, while another would paint the Mona Lisa? Obviously it's possible that the husband says he's going for a bike ride and kills himself three houses down the road. The likeliest outcome, what ends up happening, in fact, is the very thing that couldn't possibly happen. How can it be, he falls out of love, I fell out of love. We've arrived, enough time wasted on words, there's something more important than words. The towering waves crashing against the sea wall welcome us, the rocky coast gives way to the ocean landscape. I find them a pink and gold cake in the only bakery and we walk down some stairs to the sand covered in those transparent egg capsules. Happy birthday brothers, happy happy on your day, and they blow out the candles. The sea, mom! They say mom so naturally now. We climb onto the pier, then jump from rock to rock until we reach the last one. From there we see the lighthouse turn on. I picture myself climbing up the iron ladder, finding the key and staying there to live in the breakwater. I put the tent up between the rocks and we doze. When they wake up they look at me and in unison they say, who are you? What do you mean who am I? Who else would I be? Neither of them can sleep, we end up tossing and turning, it's all very eerie. Before they would've spent the afternoon throwing snowballs in the garden and then made pancakes, but in the evening, while the husband went to pick up the takeout from the new neighborhood restaurant, the mother slowly strangled the three children one by one in the basement of their house in Massachusetts, she seemed particularly serene that day.

The hares devoured, the digestif, cognac, Armagnac, calvados, aged rum, since it didn't occur to anyone in the family to have children, since there is nobody at the short-legged table, nobody with a high-pitched voice, nobody innocent and everyone here has been alive for over half a century, everything is on the brink of collapse. We drink, A doesn't touch me when his parents are around, he won't adjust my shoulder straps or brush up against my legs either. I don't know what they're talking about, the mother is making jokes about how quickly the son grew, from one minute to the next he had a bulge, a chin, he's unrecognizable or disfigured. They were telling stories about May '68, about nudism. I want to know what's special about me. There's nothing special about you, don't you worry about that, the mother-in-law says, we've seen many come and go before you and we'll see many more after you. What do you mean you will see many more? My boyfriend doesn't move, they serve him his aperitif, he stands and brings over the cinnamon puff pastries, no that's for the dessert table, take it away, the mother tells him.

My boyfriend takes them away again and he just stands there, sit down, they tell him. Do you have birthmarks? I look at myself, I try to cover myself, stretch the material, my boyfriend is still silent, he is looking at a horse out the window. They're freckles I was born with, my whole family has them. Turning away from me she says the freckles are typical of diaspora families and that's how they can recognize us. Is your hair red all over? Does the carpet match the drapes, the father-in-law asks. Father, stop, my boyfriend says, why don't we talk about politics instead? You're both thoroughly French too, including your noses.

We miss daddy, one of them says, I can't tell which one. They aren't identical twins, I am constantly having to clarify. You miss daddy now? And why do you miss daddy if I'm here? Am I not enough? But we're going on adventures to the sand dunes, to see colossal waves, I give you everything that could possibly be given, why would you say that you miss him? What other little boys get to sleep in a car, get to live a life on safari, eat just like in the movies on the side of the road and piss all over the plants? You are privileged. Everyone else has to live the life of children, which means they don't have a life at all, if you want to have fun with me I'll show you my trick for holding my breath. I breathe in and then I don't breathe out, the two of them look at me. Callac, Huelgoat, Landerneau, Daoulas, Lanvéoc, Crozon. We stop in an industrial area with roundabouts and agricultural machine hangars. We look for a place to have fun. In the distance, glory, Mount Olympus, a Burger King. Burger! We run for our meals: Big King bacon & onion XXL for E, King Wings meal for J, and the Big Fish meal for me. The boys wait for their happy meals inside a tube with a ball pit. A thin father wearing a beret next to a little girl is sitting at a nearby table. We exchange glances. Is he looking at me with desire or irritation? Does he want to grab me by the back of the neck and stick it in me after exchanging a couple of words, or is he laughing about how bulky I am? Does he see me or not? We eat, the brothers make fun of my breaded fish. Who orders fish at a Burger King? A breaded fish! A beheaded fish! I'm getting more and more swollen by the minute, my stomach fertilized, my armpit dripping, they too with their little fat rolls ought to go up a size, donate their clothes to refugees. The door opens, two police officers come in, the third is locking the patrol car outside. The boys have their backs turned to the door, licking ketchup off their fingers. A man looks at the ticket order numbers on the screen, the father and little girl finish their meals, he strokes her head with his greasy hand. The last police officer comes in smiling, the other two are already walking around the family tables. On an impulse I take our trays and move to another table. The brothers don't understand, I sit them down in front of the man and his little girl. When the police officers stop and take notice, we are a family. The man and his little girl lean back, don't worry it's all good and I rearrange the trays on the table, let's go guys, all three of you, your food will get cold. Lovely day for an outing, don't you think? The man takes hold of his daughter's hand. I'm sorry, do I know you? I stroke the man's cheek, thinking it might work, the police officer is observing the scene in the coastal region's fast food chain, we remind him of his ex. But everything happens in less than a second, the man aggressively pushes my hand off his face and hisses are you deranged, madam? What's going on, sir, asks the youngest police officer. I have two options, but I can only see one. And I throw myself onto his face and stick my tongue into his mouth, so that everything is quickly funneled into the unseemly realm of the domestic dispute. Another option, deny everything, I didn't touch him, you're the one who was staring at me and making obscene gestures, that's why I came over here, to give him what he had coming, you don't do that to mothers, not with young children around. I bite him while the police officers consult their radios. What's going on madame? Was this man bothering you? Nothing, officer, we were having an argument, my husband can't control himself and then it's always the same, she was asking for it, same old story. Get this crazy woman out of here, please! Sir, calm down, have some respect for the mother of your children, another officer says. The man gets up and throws a punch, the officers restrain him then take him away, the girl is left alone and she looks at me, but in the end it's just another violent love scene. The man handcuffed in the patrol car, the officers order caramel ice creams. The minute they drive away, we bolt. Those organized suburban guerrillas that plunder this country with their disdain for the West capture the attention of the Civil Guard and the officers, leaving us mothers in peace.

My lawyer has dropped me, a letter of resignation, it was time. I drive to the point where the map shows the edge of the seaside resort facing the virgin island of Morgat. In the distance a warm, dry storm of sand and wind, like in the Sahara, like in the high deserts of Arabia. I leave the car on a slope, empty it, and I ask them to stand back. I move the handbrake to a halfway position, the sandy ground will give way and it will plunge down, nose first. Mom look at the twisted boats, it looks like they're eating water. Are we going to get on that ferry? That's the surprise I had prepared for you. Let's go together to buy the tickets, wait, mom is counting the bills, we make piles of coins and we buy three one-way tickets. We take a photo of ourselves, we have an hour left until the ferry leaves. A poster banning access to the virgin island, another poster warning of falling rocks and mudslides. The children easily slip under the fence and slide down to the white sand, I have to make more of an effort to reach the golden ring. I see them climbing up vines, swinging, they are two albino monkeys at risk of extinction.

A: Are you in France?

L: Why?

J & E: Yes, daddy, we're here, we're two albino monkeys!

A: What do you mean albino monkeys? What's going on?

L: Go and play and you can talk more afterwards.

A: Where are you going?

L: Then they've gone.

A: Do you know what's going to happen when they find you?

L: Danger is always just around the corner, nothing happens on vacation until an alligator eats the dog.

A: Your lawyer called, she offered to help me.

L: Solidarity among women, alive and well.

A: She offered to find them.

L: Women hating women.

A: Just tell me where and I'll go.

L: How many witnesses do you have?

A: A lot more than before. They went to your house.

L: I imagined they would, I hope they watered the plants.

A: You took things of mine.

L: How did you become an enemy?

A: There are enemies everywhere, Lisa.

L: You can take every last thing in that house, you can burn it down as revenge.

A: You can come back, we were able to save it, this is your home.

L: I'll need to consult with my lawyer.

A: Your lawyer joined our team.

L: I'll find another one.

A: You're going to turn up at a police station with two kidnapped children?

A: Hello?

L: What guarantees do I have?

A: Anything you want.

L: I'll have to consult with someone.

A: Your lawyer is here with me, ask her.

L: We start again, but if it doesn't work, will you grant me a divorce?

A: Let's not assume the worst, I love you, even more than before.

I run along the sand dunes, I throw myself on top of the brothers. The wind cracks the glass of one of my lenses, I stick it back in the best I can. I have something to tell you, daddy's coming, he's on his way! Yaaay, they jump up and down on the sand, yaaay, the three of us jump and spin on the scoria. Now you really have to behave yourselves because daddy's coming. We will be ready for him, clean and perfumed inside the car among rosemary, palm, and coconut trees. Earlier they climbed up so high that they made a coconut fall, and we managed to crack open. And how do I know you won't come with the police? I'm not coming with the police. I haven't told anyone, I didn't leave any clues. Everyone is having a nap, the shutters are drawn, you know what it's like, it's quiet at this time of day. If you don't trick me, you can see them, if not, you know what will happen. I'm coming as fast as I can, two tickets already for speeding around Le Mans with those cameras and three points off the license. I should smash all those speed cameras with rocks.

For two hours I signaled to him that I wanted to leave, but nothing. I looked out of the window, I didn't dare to leave alone. Of course it's all the politicians' fault but the immigrants are fast approaching the immorality of Sodom and Gomorrah, the downward spiral is going to catch up with us. It already has, we're in free fall, it's too late. We don't have a minute to spare, soon we'll see the first flicker of fire and brimstone from heaven. They are blasphemous and bloodthirsty, but who's to blame? Not them, to hell with them, it's us. I began to feel as if I were at a burial, I wanted to leave but the only way out was with him. It was already dark, we hadn't gotten up from the table all day and nobody was even going to the toilet. Bladders and bowels exploding underneath leather clothing. Let's go, let's go, I said to him under my breath, but he didn't react, I'm tired, let's leave. France is destined to be walled off. My mother-in-law heard me and tells the aunt with the shaved head. She wants to take him away already, she tries to snatch him in the middle of the gathering, always with the excuse that she's tired. Both of them are beyond tipsy and encourage me to drink alcohol and I pour out all the bottles, I'm in the middle of my fertility treatment. This wasn't a family gathering, it was a political meeting, they weren't going to succeed, I acted as though I was drinking, as though I was on their side, but I was somewhere else, imagining what was going on with my ovarian reserve. No babies? I'm undergoing treatment, and they smiled at one another. We are born with three hundred thousand follicles but only four hundred reach maturity and expel their egg from the first time you menstruate until menopause, it's a race that's simultaneously utopian and hopeless. Suddenly the hands of all the respectable family members began to move. Hands like tarantulas underneath the table. I stood up, my ovaries were hurting, it could mean bad news or it could be a good sign that my ovaries were working. It's not the immigrants' fault, the West is falling, our rural world failed to build a legacy, but their civilized world is murderous too, everything will end in spectacular collapse. Open up your folding chairs to watch the asteroid fall and hit the West. Tell her to stop talking so much!, said the mother-in-law, go on my love, son, bring more small crystal glasses. Putin is right, the West is crumbling. Enough about Putin, who is Putin, down with Putin, she shouted.

You're not going to believe this, I'm driving past the beach with the tangled seaweed, where you were jealous of my friend who sunbathed topless and would press her nipples against the rocks in Montpellier. Everything is covered in seaweed now, it's all in the past, the strangling against the door one Christmas with my grandparents in Bourges, it's all in the past, the seaweed on the shore. I want to look after you, I've always looked after you, but now I'm going to be a man and we're going to be a family, and families don't abandon each other, we can't abandon love, whether they like it or not, do you hear me? Yes, I tell him, no more assaults when you come back from the casino all sweaty, when I have to go to the shed to smell the clothes you scattered across the lawn. I can't wait to see you, me neither.

We had two sons born in the same minute, one head came out, and then the other one fell out. But before that I used to search for him in the village, begging all the neighbors, who said they hadn't seen him, we only have an hour left to try, please, did you see him at the aqueduct, the tennis court, the airfield runway? We only have an hour and he runs away, I would go to my parents-in-law's house, she would hide him, I would see her walking around through the living room windows, but when I went in, there was no sign of her, she would leave through the greenhouse and hide among her roses and marigolds. My mother-in-law would stash her son away in the attic, where they would watch Austrian films from her licentious youth, lying on the reindeer hide rug surrounded by record players. Don't you want descendants? What about the Fournier name when you're all on your deathbeds? I'm past the forty-year mark, if you don't help me find your son right now, you'll be to blame if I get a hemorrhage or if my placenta detaches. But she wouldn't say a word, her lips curled inwards as if she were toothless. She knew exactly where she'd put him, there were many hiding places in the house and her son is a needle, he could fit into any trunk, under the desk, camouflaged between cushions on a landing, behind the curtains like a mannequin. At seven thirty in the evening, dinner and the questions: How's the treatment going? Is it working? To spell out the fact that my biology was a disaster and we were headed straight for the firing line. The next day at the moment of the upward curve I would once again be pursuing him and the neighbors were his allies, has nobody seen him?

We kiss, we embrace, we kiss again with the taste of smoke. Are the boys in the car? He looks in the window, he's dazzled by the headlights, he searches the floors, under the seats, in the trunk. Where did you put them? Calm down, they're around. But where exactly? Around. But where? What's going on? We embrace, our bodies pressed together. I'm seeing something new in his eyes at this very moment: he thinks I've done something to them. He thinks I'm capable but he doesn't want to reveal his fear. Swamps and peaks of terror, pretend there's nothing wrong so the other doesn't blow a fuse. First I needed to know your intentions, I couldn't risk being ambushed. Do I look like I have bad intentions? Do you see my lawyers here? They're here, boys, come out, your father doesn't believe me! And they come out from behind a huge palm tree and the four of us jump up and down. I'm so happy, he says, I'm so happy, I say, everyone's happy, they say.

I left my parents-in-law's house, I went back, retracing my footsteps one by one. I was terrified of being alone on the other side of the door, on the side that belonged to nature, to livestock, and everything that happens while we're sleeping, pursuit, depravity. When we wake up, the animals are asleep, we never find out what really happened, but imagine if someone were to climb to the top of a tower and see the night with their own eyes. They were having so much fun on the other side of the glass, they were playing a lewd game of charades. Suddenly the family home was a secret committee. Don't lie, we all know your thoughts on the subject, is she a hundred percent Jewish? What do you mean a hundred percent? She must have some impure ancestors, mixed ones, don't you think? Let her husband speak, he's the one who knows, the husband who traveled so far, all the way to the other side of the Atlantic to find what was right in front of him, he chose her among thousands. Mother, please, why must you meddle with my life? I'm not meddling, I'm giving you my opinion. Perhaps my son didn't realize, it's not something you notice at first sight, and then falling in love is a fatwa. But what is it that he didn't see?, asks the uncle, I had a very good friend who was one of them and it was never an issue with her. His wife swivels her head like an ostrich, asks him which very good friend because she's never met his very good friend. The uncle doesn't reply. Shhh, she left but she could have come back. Tell us, tell us. Leave me alone, what do you want me to say? She's just one of them, that's all. It's not even obvious, nobody can tell. My son is a good man, I raised him well, in a good family, I'm proud, bravo, we mustn't discriminate. Is she a member of a sect? Of course she is, says the aunt, still unsettled by her husband's mysterious very good friend. I'm not saying she's different because she's one of them, I'm saying that for a life to progress normally, to avoid tragedies, it won't be the same, everything will be rougher for them. Is her entire family tree Israelite? Does she celebrate rituals with bearded men? I've heard they purify themselves in water before coitus. I've heard they practically cut the firstborn son's whole penis off, even more than the Muslims do. I've heard they wear wigs and never wash their private parts, that they smell like cooking oil.

I don't know if it's the stridulating of the crickets, or the roiling waves advancing towards the shore, but it gets dark. Let's go out to eat, it's on me, you're my family, he declares with pride. Is this how you've all been dressed since you left? I picture my mother-in-law, Madame S, washing, drying, perfuming our clothes, bringing it all over, impeccable, leaving the pile on the little entrance table, leaving without making a sound, without me noticing she's still behind the folding screen. I sit down in the passenger seat. The boys get in, dressed however they please. Who in this family likes a rainstorm?, asks dad. Who likes scuba diving more than anything else in the world? Me, they shout with collective euphoria, me, although they don't know what it is. Who wants to travel in a submarine more than anything else in the world? Me, we all say, although I have no idea what it would be like to breathe in a submarine.

Everything was intensely dark, but the birds and the sounds of them scolding one another kept me company. At home, the traces of the father-in-law's fall were waiting for me. I had an idea, maybe another test would ease my anxiety. I'd bought them in bulk and had hidden them in pouches wrapped in towels under the bed. Sitting on the toilet, my genitals exposed, I saw just one line, I hadn't been impregnated. With child, expecting, as my mother-in-law described her time with my boyfriend inside her. Could it be a false negative? Do I have too few hormones circulating in my blood, is it too soon, had they put alcohol in my glass? I'll wait two more days. I destroy the test and throw it into the trash can with yesterday's dinner, who cares if I have one child, two children, three children, four children, tyrants have a thousand children, who the fuck needs children, the only thing you need is fury, in giving birth, in aborting, whatever. I hear the door, he comes in swaying, behind him his uncle and his father help keep him steady and they take off his shoes. The three of them look at me without understanding what's going on, holding each other up, the three village stooges. Call the mother-in-law and the aunt, I have incredibly important news! Outside, the day had appeared like an intruder, the deer and snakes were escaping through the tall weeds and nobody had slept. Your mother-in-law passed out on the kitchen countertop, the uncle tells me, we have to let her rest, the aunt ended up face down on the living room carpet. They got out of there, leaving my husband with his trousers around his ankles.

The food spins around on a hotplate, we grab it with our hands, our bellies swollen, we play I spy, the yes or no game, we keep adding forbidden words, we play another one that involves experiments inside the glasses using the spicy sauces. We play Simon says, but the French version: De Gaulle says, we play who can catch the fattest fish. The plates spin and we get dizzy. I eat something violet, pink, red, something emerald green, I eat cacti implanted in the desert. The boys put everything in their mouths, saffron, korma curry, mountains of mango. Eating is so hypnotic, like those fields filled with gleaming yellow flowers that are about to start rotting. The boys were as hungry as bears too, look my love, now they're trying to stick their hands into the fish tanks and trap the koi. We go out, the boys watch us smoke together, they squeeze between us like in a ventilation duct, they're inside our nuclear reactor. We let them try a few puffs, just like in the old days when nobody said anything and children smoked like chimneys.

He hits the brakes like an acute myocardial infarction. He pushes the seat back, he kisses me, I can't see anything, it's like kissing a stranger, an American black bear. He whimpers a confession I've heard before, about who he wanted to be before he met me, a French volleyball champion, before his parents and I broke him down. He whimpers about moving houses when he was born, from one caravan to the next with a lazy father, always suffering, and ending up in Lot's desolate campgrounds. The hidden river that would drag the children who behaved badly to its depths. The wild moans of the mother with strange men whose cowboy boots clicking against the floor was the only noise he ever heard them make. Father and son in folding chairs listening to the volatile mother's shrieks, and then the three of them having dinner together, a barbecue and bottles of barley water surrounded by nature. Occasionally father and son escape to see the Croatian circus. The father was much older, the father dreaming of being a high-ranking military man, an air-force general, starfleet admiral, playing at guerrilla warfare in the circus tent, begging to be hired. The father who would say: never trust a woman who makes your hands shake. You remember? The first time we saw each other my hands shook. Lisa, when we go back I can buy mortar, lime, cement, gravel and build the upstairs floor, I'll do it all by myself. The hot desert of my childhood, waking up and not knowing where I slept, the men lined up, ready. This addiction has to be fought because after a drop comes a sip, then a glass, a bottle, and finally alcohol poisoning. The boys are here, in the back with their eyes shut on their parents' love. We get to the bungalow he reserved, talking about his parents brought him back to life. Stop now, I tell him in language that the law can understand, stop right in the middle of the act, it's like stopping a high-speed train with your own throbbing hands. Who can ask that of a man, he says. So this is rape now? I don't want you to turn around and say I abused you. We keep making love. How can there be a rape between a married couple in a shared bed under the same roof? How can one tongue assault another? What will they think of next? Tell me how it's possible to legislate against such a thing. If that exists, then anything can exist, every form of love is a violation because we can never really know a thing about what the other person wants. Besides, wait, there's no struggle, I could prove it, vaginal fluid can be proven in court by experts. Nothing can be proven, that's the problem with everything, desire, the lack of desire, it's impossible to prove. We'd made up by the time we finished having sex. I didn't understand what you were asking me, were you asking me for love? You didn't want it? You let me do it. Could you stop or not? Do you know anyone physically capable of slamming on the brakes on a downward slope without breaking their neck?

The next day the visitors and the locals sleep for twenty-four hours, it looks like a Ku Klux Klan massacre. My parents-in-law, the aunts and uncles and my boyfriend sleep soundly, they stink, their greasy hair flat against their scalps. I sleep intermittently and I wake up with a start thinking that the test was a false negative. I root around in the trash, I find it, I still think it's very odd that I'm not pregnant after so much passion and perseverance. What if he's slipping me some chemical that makes his sperm reject my egg? What if that's why the gametes aren't meeting? Why isn't my little egg fertilized in my tube, why isn't it moving towards my uterus? Is it because I'm forty years old or above and it doesn't reach my uterus in time to implant itself? I stare at my boyfriend's face, and when he opens one eye, I tell him in a calm tone: today we are going to tell them the news. He doesn't grasp my words, in general he doesn't grasp anything, even if he's sober. The news: yesterday's test was positive, we did it, we will give this village of octogenarians a child. I make him two black coffees. A little while later we knock on the parents-in-law's door and go inside without waiting for them to open it. Inside: sparkling wreaths, Napoleon Bonaparte's cognac glasses, the rococo furniture, high heeled shoes on the wall-to-wall carpet, croissants on a small porcelain plate. We have some very important news: a Jew is going to join the family.

It doesn't matter what happens during these hours, nothing will be useful for a judge, there are no witnesses, there are no informants, there is no paperwork, we all agreed to come, it's his word against mine, his right to reply against mine. Four people from the same family are laid out in different rooms, they'll say as they enter the house cordoned off with yellow tape. Love is willful devastation, a network of pedophiles, a legal scandal in a provincial court. Love is bribery in the plain light of day, a padlocked emergency exit, fireworks aimed at the sky. Love is a fated journey, a genetically modified face. I pushed him into the river for love. I did what I did in the name of *love*. I molested her because I loved her too much, being her father wasn't enough, conventional love wasn't enough, because conventional love isn't enough for anybody. Love is the ultimate defenselessness. I wake up the next day, I try to reconstruct the day before, reconstruct last night's argument, how did we get here, what's the collateral damage, how are we planning to survive, what's our life expectancy. Panic if he took my papers and ran away with them. I don't even remember what we said to each other yesterday, how far we took it with our words, if one of us shattered a glass over the other's head, if they saw something out of the ordinary. The boys aren't in their beds but I can see his foot, he's asleep. I open the door to the cold and sunny morning, they're playing without their coats on the wooden terrace, I hug them, I tell them that mom loves them more than anyone, I try to avoid all artifice and affectation, so that they feel the love exactly as it is, but I don't know exactly what this love is. The father wakes up, the boys run to greet him, I love you more than anyone, he tells them, but that missile was aimed at me. The four of us have breakfast, the bungalow includes a family breakfast, pass me the croissant, here's your coffee, the boys guzzle down the boiling milk, their father spreads butter on their toast, he shows them how to write the alphabet backwards, he trims their fingernails. What a disaster, he says. We were running away, not on an island vacation, I tell him, did you want me to cut their fingernails on the road, while I was driving? He puts their black fingernail clippings on the table. Look at them, they're like horse's hoofs. And what are you trying to say? He stands up, just look at the state of them when they're with their mother. Don't say that in front of them, don't put ideas in their heads. You do that all by yourself, you dig your own holes. We keep eating breakfast, nobody stands up, inside me there's a flood, a demolished dam, something impossible. I can't do this. What can't you do? Well, let me explain, you're going to have to, because otherwise they're going to take them away from you again, if that's not already happening. You took them away from me, I just obeyed. Really, you think obeyed is the right word? Breakfast is finished, he gets them ready. I put the boys in my car and sit in the driver's seat, he gestures for them to get into his car, but I start the engine and go, follow me. Nobody has their seat belts on, the doors are open, I close them as I'm driving, before they fall into the ditch. There's a voice telling me to plan a day at the seaside, a picnic, a trip to the aquarium, a theme park. Another voice is telling me I have to follow my gut and resolve this situation before darkness falls on us like a knife. He follows us, we move in a slow convoy like a small trailer carrying livestock. At the roundabouts we circle around several times like a herd on its way to the slaughterhouse, weighing up whether or not to escape and free the beasts along the way or finish them off. I'll tell him to forget all about yesterday, we should try, Michel and Monique, the diabolical couple, joining forces. We must look like we're on drugs, he shouts at me through the window, they're going to take them from us, they love reporting people here and Child Protection Services is always lurking. They're not enacting a systematic plan to steal babies, here they do it for the infants' own good, but either way it's stealing. Let's go somewhere, anywhere, we're hungry now, say E and J. Hold on, hold on. I get a feeling that we're surrounded by countless enemies.

They look at me, their eyes bulging. The mother-in-law asks the son if it's true that a Jew is going to join the family. The son looks at me, he isn't sure about anything either, I tell her yes, that she should be asking me, that I am the pregnant one. Or did you forget that we have ovaries and eggs? How passé!, said the aunt. Luckily, the mother-in-law added: that's the last thing we need, those predators carrying a baby for nine months, men aren't capable of anything, let alone carrying something inside their bodies. I also think we men are predators, dear wife of mine, said the father-in-law, thank goodness for women. A miracle occurs: my mother-in-law pounced on me, her makeup streaked with tears. We start dancing and I show her some rikudim steps. And what the hell is this, they say, their arms up in the air, a tribal dance? A Zulu ceremonial dance? It's rikudim, I tell them, and get them all to dance.

We're a Texan family, we're surrounded by jungle and the Río Bravo on the United States border. Should we go to the Houston Space Center to see the interactive exhibitions designed by NASA? He looks at me like I've really lost my mind and reevaluates the option of swift action with the help of sedatives. The waitress is a sexy cowgirl, wow, aren't they all good-looking. Where are you from? We ask them for the "holdup" meals and mac and cheese. He touches my waist, he puts his arm around my shoulders, you'll see the new life that could be yours if you stick it out with us. J and E put coins into the claw machines with stuffed animals. A poster warns of the risk of epilepsy triggered by the hypnotic machine and its fluorescent lights. They come and go, asking for more coins, they pound on the glass, they have fun trying to push it over. How nice to have children you can throw coins at like a queen in colonial times. Between the two of them they manage to get the metal claw to grab hold of the head of a rhinoceros and they get it to drop into the hole. They try to crawl into the hole, they get stuck, they're hired as stuffed animals for the rest of their lives and no longer have to live with us and one day the metal claw grabs them and delivers them to a different family. They celebrate with a hug, jumping up and down and running back to the table holding the rhinoceros up like a trophy. We look at them like two boys left on the doorstep of the CPS building. The sexy waitress arrives with the food, nobody speaks, our teeth are covered in cheddar, nobody looks at anybody, nobody cares about anybody. We're an obese family, I bite, swallow and in that moment he grabs my hand and places it on his swollen thigh. I leave my hand there and keep adding to the weight of desire. He nods towards where he wants us to go, I know what the bathrooms are like in these places. I look at the boys eating and laughing with their cheese-smeared rhinoceros. I want to follow him, but I don't want them to give us dirty looks, for them to kick down the door and find us there covered in blood. The waitress brings them little toys and puzzles. He pulls down my flowery dress that's bursting at the seams, I look down at the rolls of my stomach, fuck, I'm still hungry, so hungry. We hold the door closed with a foot, we do it quickly, I walk out packed with sperm inside me like an overstuffed suitcase before a long journey. The table is strewn with our coats, wallets, and toys, but they aren't there. I search for them all around the restaurant, playing the distracted mother: little ones, boys, J, E, J, E, I call them in a singsong voice and pretend we're playing hide and seek, as though I haven't lost them. Two managers in Christmas-red uniforms glare at me coldly from behind the counter. I smile at them, trying to win them over, disoriented: have you seen them around here? One gives me a dirty look. Is that them? They point at two fifteen-year-olds poking one another with wire contraptions. No, I say, do they look like children to you? Do you think I could be their mother? If that's not them, we haven't seen them. You didn't see them running around the restaurant with a stuffed animal? Nobody came through here, madame. What do you mean nobody came through here, didn't you see a pair of twins playing with the stuffed animal machine? What machine, madame? There is no stuffed animal machine here. A comes out of the toilet. They aren't here, I tell him, and these two are trying to confuse me by saying there aren't any stuffed animals. Armand confronts them, did you tell her there was no stuffed animal machine when we can see a fucking stuffed animal machine right in front of you? The employee smiles, I hadn't understood what she said, sir. A grabs his head and smashes his face into the machine. The two of us walk between the customers swearing and looking underneath the tables, behind the stack of baby high chairs, in the kitchen with the immigrants in their plastic caps and ground meat on their hands. It went wrong. A goes outside to search the surrounding industrial area and construction sites. I'm still on all fours, praying. There's a couple at the back drinking a toast with a stroller next to them, a baby's hand raised in the air. If they don't appear, I'll abduct that baby, run away with the stroller and we can escape, I'll come out of this life with something to show for it. A victim's right to identity theft. He'll go along with it, force majeure identity swap and all set, the baby would never even know. The young couple have time to make several more and live off social services. Her ovarian reserve is probably overflowing, enough to donate eggs as a good cause. I leave the restaurant, walk around the block, I can hear him in the distance, calling them from behind a highway sign. A pink inflatable giraffe moves in the dusk light, diggers are parked between the wrecks of luxury cars. I see my J and E with their stuffed animal eating trash off the ground. We go back for the coats, they ask us to pay and leave. The waiter wipes the blood from his mouth.

We are a couple facing external threats from the south, north, east, and internally, we're capable of attacking ourselves, of turning ourselves inside out. I keep going, he signals at me to take the exit with a sign for paintball. A gift, a celebration of children's day so we have a nice time, so we can fabricate some kind of memory. So that when they interrogate the children there's something nice about us in their testimony. We spend hours shooting in the garden like the day the brother of the future king was killed, until the parents insist that the gun is locked away. After begging the mother a thousand times, the little brothers tell her it's not loaded, they just want to look at daddy's gun. Mother, please, mother, we just want to look at it, we don't want to pull the trigger. The mother of the future king believes it isn't loaded and doesn't check. The two little brothers are alone in the room, and despite the mother's highly sensitive hearing, she doesn't hear the shot. Later they'll say that while they were cleaning the revolver that night he shot himself in the forehead and died within a few minutes. It's a dark chapter in the saga of the family dynasty, involuntary homicide, there wasn't even an autopsy. I care about you so much Lisa, he says, shooting a paintball into my forehead. I care about you, I say, I care about you very much, care, sociopaths care, I love you all, he says to me, I love you all so much that I would lie down on the runway and let an airplane crush me. This is his way of convincing me that I was the one who asked to go paintballing in this field, that I'm the one who wants to go back to the village and learn to drive, that I'm the one who needs it in order to be a mother, that I grovel for love. The way, he says, you tell me that I raped you when you're the one who started it. The way he makes me believe that I can't control myself when he's the one who encourages me to lose control. The way of making me unforgivable to myself. The brothers hurl themselves around until they're exhausted, we're asked to return the guns but we all keep shooting, first with paint, then without any cartridges. Bang bang bang, we throw ourselves behind wooden ramparts. Bang bang bang, behind parapets. Sir, madam, we are closing, do you understand? You must hand over the weapons and go to the changing rooms. Bang bang bang, all four of us shoot.

My false pregnancy was discovered sooner than I expected thanks to the town gossips. I used to walk through the village pushing out my belly in elastic trousers and rubber shoes, greeting the neighbors who would touch my belly with nothing inside but gastric juices and air. The idea was to run with the announcement all the way, until I really was pregnant, and nobody would bother to calculate the date afterwards. The problem was how to keep actively trying to get pregnant, since I supposedly already was, but now that the pressure had been taken off, he was suddenly insatiable and didn't run away so often to the sheds, I would take full advantage and lift my legs up for half an hour afterwards. The mother-in-law looked for baby clothes that were neither pink nor blue until she knew the sex, many afternoons I found her on the computer looking up circumcision and the possible risks of blood loss or hemorrhage, and she'd tell her son about the barbarity of the practice. One day Gilbert, the only dancer in the village, told another neighbor that he saw my negative pregnancy tests, his Pomeranian found them in my trash. One after another, the senile couple, Nadia and her red-haired daughter, the agoraphobic neighbor who lives with reptiles, they exposed me. They got together, they lifted up my T-shirt and there were tears, screams of hatred, but also celebrations for the son that wouldn't be born.

A: Well, well, our little family is going home, they're going to welcome us back like cycling champions.

L: Where?

A: At the entrance of the village. Don't make me nervous, I have to drive a long way and one of our lights is out. You've been hopping around like the rabbits you found on the other side of the pond, now it's time to go. This time they're getting in with me.

L: But they've been riding with me.

A: I'm not the one who crashed into a truck at the Forêt de Prémery curve and had to have my parents come and rescue them.

L: Why didn't you come and rescue me?

A: Don't make me ask them who they would rather ride with.

I take them by the arm, one in each hand, two crutches, two orthopedic shoes. Armand takes them from me, he grabs them tight and pulls them towards his body. The sun is a black ball, the fireflies are the only source of light. I didn't want to shout like that, not right off the bat, but I do it, they're coming with me. I couldn't take the risk of having to follow them through tunnels and then losing sight of them in a zigzag. The boys say they can't see anything and that it's fun, I pull them loose from the father's grip. He brings his head right up close to mine, as if to knock me out. It wouldn't be so bad to die on the pavement at a shooting range. I'm not giving in, I am their mother. Oh, he laughs, don't make me laugh, I am their mother, I am their mother, as if that ever meant anything, go ahead and tell me another joke. Who could possibly comprehend all the things you've done since the day they were born? They're coming with me and we'll stop halfway, if they want to switch cars then you can take them, OK? I propose we do it the other way around. They come with me and halfway, if they want, they go with you. Or let's ask them, but I don't think it's going to go your way: boys, come here, boys! Who would you rather travel home with? Answer the question instead of pretending to be terrified, it's terrifying, but it's going to be great, just tell us now. He grabs me by the neck, it's been so long since he did it that I'd forgotten the shock of being lifted up like a swan. Like a cabriole, a fantastic leap with a majestic twirl on the opening night of the opera, he lifts me up by the neck, we go from affectionate inertia straight to the act. My feet in the air, he drops me and I fall. Leave them with me, I tell him, and I'll come home. Come home, either way you're coming home, what other option do you have, besides collecting trash on the highway and calling it art. The boys pretend to run a sack race through the fog, we trap them like flies to throw into the fire. He puts them inside his car and shuts the automatic doors.

When it was finally positive, I jumped up and down like a cheerleader, I went running around the riverbanks, I celebrated by lighting candles, but I didn't say anything to anyone, not to the father, I didn't tell a soul and not a single neighbor found out that my period of mourning had come to an end. I pulled if off, avoiding any more embarrassing scenes. The village still had no infants in sight, the neighbors were happy that way, because it meant no irritating childish noise, no little cars littering the landscape, no pedophiles circling the area in white vans. I wore clothes in size XXL from the very beginning, went out very little or only late at night, hid my cravings and continued to drink beer and aperitifs in public. Gilbert thought it was strange that he never saw me, Nadia and her daughter also wondered why I stopped going by their house to eat junk food and listen to sixties music, but I told everyone I needed time for introspection and spirituality and everyone wet themselves laughing; time for what? I began collecting toys that belonged to children who left everything behind in their houses when they moved away, children who'd been strangled in caves, unborn children whose junkie mothers had prepared altars for them. I collected donations, cans of powdered milk, baby accessories, everything went in the attic, or old closets. I went to my checkups by train or hitchhiked to the closest hospital. Once I was too swollen I invited him to the Pougues-les-Eaux casino to have dinner and gamble and I told him the news as we were drinking our aperitifs, an olive on the rim of the Jerez glass. I told him about feto-placental circulation, how the cardiovascular system works, how I was creating a neural tube. He played a slot machine, hey, are you listening, a life, it's a life, a life that might be fully lived, a whole century. What you do here every night isn't a game, it's an addiction that's paving the way to criminality, hey, I'm here growing slabs of tissue, muscles, and soon, believe it or not, Schwann cells, meninges, melanocytes, adrenal medulla, and bones. Who's Schwann? Probably one of your Israeli friends. To boost my ego I added: and soon the fingers and the toes, sexual organs, and eyelashes! That night we competed at chugging our drinks, he spent his entire instructor's salary, finding out he was going to be a father hit him like a punch in the face, so I told him there was only one. But once we were in the car I blurted out that they were twins. That night we drove into the village honking the horn like Moors at the climax of a wedding feast, until a hidden police car at a roundabout saw us. They chased us, they made him take a breathalyzer test, which came out much higher than 0.8, and they took away his license.

The three of them drive cautiously across an open field until they turn onto the Iroise coastal road, the far west. It's a small inland sea, at this hour it was violet, fluorescent with glowworms among the sharks. Boys, look at the violet water, I said, even though they couldn't hear me. It's not violet, it's neon green, one of them replies inside my head, where's mom going?, they shout. I cry as we take a shortcut through acacia and eucalyptus trees but nobody will believe me, they'll say it's just a ruse to get them back. As I follow them I regret not having fought harder, even if he had to run me over with his Mégane. I want to listen to "Amor Fati," love, pretend to be Cantat, imitate his movements, cold-blooded slaughter in Vilnius, I want a panic button, Prelude and Fugue No. 2 in C Minor, BWV 847, makes me feel like I'm going to puke and I switch it off. They're right about that, I'm a fake writer, nobody believes anything I say about wanting to write something one day, I don't even believe it myself. I call him, he doesn't pick up. I call again. Voicemail. What game is he playing now, I call again and he's turned off his phone. We've emptied more than half the tank already, we'll have to stop at a gas station. I honk the horn, it's useless, I pull up close behind him, my windshield gets covered in dirt. Hey! I try to pull up alongside him but the road is too narrow. Can you brake? Can you shift down a gear? I want to jump into his car at full speed like in action movies when they leap from a moving airplane onto a semitrailer on a bridge. Can you hear me? It's pointless, the race continues off-road, to think he accused me of never taking my foot off the accelerator. It goes on like this for hours, me behind him glancing up at the moon so the sun doesn't rise.

Occasionally, my brain is plagued by the thought: he's no longer ahead of me, it's just a shadow, I've lost them in the clusters of trees. They're my children, blood is thicker than water. He's making me suffer, I'm close to the shoulder, he won't let me pass on the left or the right, he rolls down his window, he shows me something, I can't quite make it out, it looks like a gun. We carry on like this, who knows for how long, again he sticks something out the window, it's a gun, is it real? Does it have rubber or lead bullets? Until suddenly something makes him slow down, there's no space to decelerate, I slam on the brakes. He stumbles down the side of the road, keeps going until he reaches a tree, unzips his pants and starts pissing, aiming very high. He doesn't turn around, he leaves his door open, the quicksand is ready to swallow me up. No child lock on the back doors, I pull out the closest body, I run to my car, place it inside, I sprint back like I'm in an Olympic race to fetch the second body, I don't know which one I'm missing, but he turns around and aims his stream at me. I don't care if I'm covered in piss, he doesn't realize I've taken one, he doesn't zip up his pants, I'm not able to steal the second, he gets into the car and accelerates. His face belongs to someone else, how different a husband's expression can be when he's alone.

The family between my bleeding legs. As if we were in an underground gambling den or a cockfight in the barren Mexican wastelands. They muttered under their breath that something strange would come out, nobody dared to say deformed. Everyone was waiting to hear the heartbeat, the first, the second, checking to see they had all their limbs and well-proportioned heads. Everyone paying close attention to the skin color because they're all for universalism and multiculturalism but not when it comes to their own families. Once I was in bed I saw my mother-in-law lean over the transparent cribs, gaze at the twins and drool.

We left Carcassonne, the babies still with their flattened skulls, we stopped to fill up with gas, we were fighting in the service station, I can't remember why, what it was that enraged us so much, I was wearing those trousers with the elastic waistband, I remember him saying I would never be a famous artist, that it wasn't a good idea, that I would be the kind that imitates reality but make it worse, that pretends to be crazy to create demented art and ends up ruining everything: the work and their lives. The babies' unfastened seat belts, the squawk of birds opening their beaks far away, the sound of a chainsaw cutting down trees. On that journey home from our vacation we took all our clothes off in one of those family hotels with a kitchen while the babies slept in their car seats on the floor like two little recently laid eggs. I can't remember why we screamed at one another, even when we were already naked, I told him that he took advantage of me, that he was suffocating me, that he wanted to set me off, he said that I was going to scam him, that he was certain I was already planning a scam coordinated from afar, perhaps my Argentine family whom he knew nothing about was behind it, perhaps they were conspiring with my religious community in Latin America. Why don't I know anything about your family? Are they traffickers? Why do you eavesdrop on our family conversations pretending to be asleep? It's suspicious that they've never come to visit, have they ever been on an airplane? Are they obsessed with visas? The bed moved, the two eggs did too. All of that has been wiped, what remains is the back of the chair with our clothes strewn over it, a song in the car as we left that hotel, the sun on the wall while we were having sex.

He's just realized, I can see him gesticulating, the shouting, poor thing, he's missing one, I'm missing one too, poor me. You stole him from me, bitch, he says, his mouth twisting. I didn't take anything from you, usurper. I keep him close to me like a larva for the rest of the drive. How little it all lasts, he turns, let's see if he gives up. He slows down, incredible, marvelous, a gift, will he shoot? Against all odds I get out and run towards him with open arms and he does the same, the two cars with the brothers separated at birth. We embrace, which one do you have, he laughs, J, I think, but I'm not sure, I'm not sure about anything, why did we have them, what do you mean why, we love them more than anything, without them we'd be nothing, you wanted them, and I didn't, but now I do, thank you for forcing me to become a father, I thought it would be a horror movie but thanks to you I have them, thank you for raping me, if you hadn't I wouldn't even be a mother, I'd just be another piece of shit in this world, it was a beautiful rape that meant I could give them to you. The car, the car! And I run to pull up the handbrake. And now what? Do you have a gun? Don't be ridiculous, it's made of plastic, I saw it, you had one! No, what an idiot, my father gave it to me, you know how he has his things, the trigger is stuck. Follow me. We can't leave the cars alone. But follow me. Where? To wherever I say, for once do as I fucking say. Don't be scared, it's a surprise, I don't want to give it away. But we can't leave them alone. Why, there's nothing here, who is going to take them, the stars? Plus, the gun will protect them. That's not funny, they could shoot each other. I told you the trigger has been stuck for fifty years. He lifts me up, throws me onto his back, and starts running. I hit his back, his neck, I make him stumble like a runner getting a cramp in the final stretch. Where are you taking me? Surprise, he says, but it sounds like survive.

Here comes the eloquent romantic from our very first nights together when we were just children, we slept in dairy farms, in castle bedchambers, in abandoned towers, we had breakfast in the stables on top of thousands of honeycombs from lost centuries and he would kiss me between the sequoias. Get down on the ground, that's an order! One of the cars moves, or at least I think it did, someone released the handbrake. I don't know if he wants to make love to me or bury me alive. Why are you filming everything? To have memories of our reconciliation. Who are you going to show it to, or sell it to? The car, I tell him, it's moving. You're seeing ghosts. Both cars now! Each one of them is inside their own black box, they must be afraid they'll die. They don't know they can die. How could they not know they could die? You don't know anything about your own children, they can't possibly know they're going to die. How stupid, it's impossible that they don't know they're going to die, the cars are shaking, let me go check. They aren't strong enough to pull up the handbrake, they can't escape. He lies on top of me on the ground covered in snails, slime, mushrooms. I feel happily harassed, I tell him, but don't film this, I don't want to see myself, I don't want you to turn me in. What exactly do you not want to see if the only person you see is yourself? You're filming everything live like a terrorist, it's pure sadism, pure cruelty. Please Lisa, don't just repeat words, there's nobody here, you're speaking for the judges, there's no signal here, it's your word against mine, neither of us could fabricate evidence. But you're still filming me, who's going to watch it? His heart fills with blood. Do you know what happened to a woman who hiked up this very mountain? I read it yesterday in the local paper. We agreed that if it came to that, we could get a divorce. We said so many things, Lisa, so many things are said over the course of a marriage, so much is said and almost none of it is true. But then you leave me with no choice. A woman your age wanted to go on a hike around here, she bought a crepe from a stand at the entrance. She was eating it as she walked in and a piece got stuck in her throat, there was nobody around, she started to cough and she choked to death on the chocolate in the crepe, they found her fifty days later. What are you trying to say? Nothing, just watch out for crepes if you go off alone in the future, but for now I'll look after you. But I want to talk about sharing the brothers. I'll finish the work on the house, I promise I'll finish the top floor, the bathtub, the railing, and we'll sell it for double. Double! But there's nothing in my name, not a single piece of paper. I turn to leave but the ground opens up beneath me. Look how hard you make me, look at how you empty out every last drop, look at your man come this hard, it must be like watching someone cry tears of blood. My hand fills with his sperm, he smears it on my face, it's much more romantic than the men who throw acid on women's faces. I have the mental age of twelve in the village, they ask me if I'm an adult before I can carry out any transaction or when I go to the supermarket, and so what, you look young. Alright fine, let's make a deal, each one of us gets back in their car and that's it, I won't take yours, you won't take mine. No, even better, let's get married again, you come home, say no more, I'll build my parents a concrete wall. This is Russian roulette with a loaded gun, a loaded gun passed back and forth from one person to the other. You really think we can live everything all over again, get married again, make twins again, aged fifty? We have no choice, we didn't leave ourselves any room to maneuver: alright, we each get one child. Are you demonic? That would traumatize them, not even monstrous parents do that, they don't even separate siblings when there's a war. And you claim to be an artist? I never said I was an artist,

I said I wanted to be something more in the future and that I could write. You pretend to be an artist with my parents and the neighbors, but there's nothing artistic about you. And you? What are you? I said that when the boys grow up, I'd like to write or do something for myself. But what exactly will you do? What could you possibly do with your life if you haven't been able to do anything so far? Nobody becomes anything just because their children grow up, let alone a writer, have you really considered that? Have you thought that maybe you just want to give them to me, get rid of them and be free? The fable of the writer killing their darlings. I twist free and run around him in the darkness like a maniacal moth. I find a large rock, he can't see me, I hide, he calls out to me: come here my little writer, my brilliant writer, and he laughs quietly, come here or I'll find you, remember I can see in the dark, remember that my eyes can see the blackness. He looks anxiously around for me, he turns back, we both turn and when I guess that he's close I throw the rock at his head and he falls. I run to his body and grab his keys. I get to his car, trembling, I open it and lift out the second unconscious body like rescuing a child from the bottom of a well.

A single objective: keep driving without the headlights. I have to find a way to slip under the radar, get away from the coast. I don't know if he's standing yet, his head bloody with a concussion, or if he's unharmed. I see the road open up in front of me, I turn off everything on the dashboard, the GPS too, I try to keep everything quiet and I step on the gas. I don't think anyone is following me, unless they're on foot, unless he manages to get up, the lid of his skull cracked open, and throw a sharp object to puncture the tires and then jump onto the hood. Unless he manages to get up, reach the gun and unlatch the safety. I turn into a narrow country lane. I decelerate, I am a slow animal, I switch off the engine, I hear nothing. Maybe he'll never wake up, maybe I didn't kill him, maybe I did and it wasn't my fault. I move the boys into a more comfortable position, one of them has a cut on his forehead, I give him sips of water, we have to survive, I wrap them up, make them a little cot, there's no movement on the horizon, I see no intruders, the trees and the ground still, the quicksand frozen stiff. There's a chance he'll manage to drag himself to the phone and call 112, he would do it just to steal the spotlight. We're going to wait, boys. I move into the back seat and I stroke them, but everything seems muddy and bleak, even when they rescue the boy in the well with a rope, they pull him up feet first and the town cheers, even there a morbid idea creeps in. When was the last time we ate a cookie, an apple, a cube of cheese? I look for something, their nerves and muscles are weak, like children just freed from a camp. Whose fault is this, just mine? Just mom's? There are so many obstacles, they jump like ring-tailed lemurs, there's something esoteric in our alliance, in being their mother. There's something esoteric with their father too, did they never notice that? Aren't they going to say anything about their father? I promise them that everything is going to change, I hear him saying from the great beyond: I'll finish all the jobs, the second floor, the railing, the bathtub and we'll sell it for double.

One afternoon I decide to open the locked doors, go outside, abandon the television and the celebrity gossip they put on for me to practice my French, and go and pick up my twins. I grab a bicycle leaning against a post in the village and pedal the five kilometers that separate us from the daycare. From the second-floor window the teacher looks surprised to see me. I'm surprised that she's surprised and she's surprised at my surprise. Has something happened? she asks, alarmed. Did something happen to them? I don't understand, they told me that you took them half an hour ago. I couldn't think clearly, I went into the main room, the other children were playing in a circle waiting for their mothers. Who took them? Who did you hand them over to? The teacher anxiously ran along the hallway and returned with the person in charge of the daycare, who confirmed that she saw with her own eyes a woman with my exact same hair come to pick them up, she didn't hesitate to hand them over when she saw how the boys ran over and hugged her. Did a sterile insane woman put my hair on her head or buy a wig in a costume to impersonate and pass herself off as me? The three of us started running around the nursery for no reason. I touched the heads of the children that looked like them, feeling an urge to kidnap one. We weren't in our right minds, the teacher said, this hasn't happened to the local daycare on a single occasion in more than one hundred years of existence, the one in charge said, we've been here since before the war. Which war? Could some degenerate be prowling around the school perimeter? Did they call her mom, my children? Yes, she nodded: I heard the word mom very clearly, this and the fact that she had, I swear to you, your exact hair, is what made me so certain that she was their mother, I mean you, that she was you. On the other hand, we've hardly seen you before. In an instant, I imagine my own mother-in-law sitting in the hairdresser trying out different hair dyes, I can see her with a goody bag in the back seat of her car. I call my boyfriend-husband, he doesn't pick up, but he never picks up when he's working or even when he's not working, sometimes I call him and someone else picks up, breathes, listens, then hangs up. Suddenly I remember how disgusted I was to find hairs in my mother-in-law's burgundy pear and cream dish. She must have been cutting something, perhaps a wig in my hair color, we were all pulling out hairs stuck to our tongues or the roofs of our mouths. I call my father-in-law, he says he's on the tractor surrounded by fallen trees and can't hear a word I'm saying. While I call my mother-in-law I let a threat fall like a guillotine onto the necks of the inept nursery managers: there will be justice.

I clean them with a wet cloth, I don't know what I've done, we need to leave the car behind, stop asking questions nobody knows the answer to. The house-on-wheels adventure is over now, we have to get all our clothes together and throw away the rest. We are already out, I ask them to say goodbye, it was our loyal companion, a horse we must put down. Get back, stay there. I leave it on a slope in first gear and we start walking, a bit further on we turn around and watch it roll towards its destruction. Bye Bye. With love, a moment comes when you don't want it to end. It's not just that the love is gone, it's that the rehearsal, the repetition, the jealousy, the sarcasm of love also disappears. We walk, the boys have grown since we left the countryside, I see them as two boy scouts pushing on toward the arid plains. We just need to get new tickets and then cross. I wonder if someone found him, if they alerted the coastal authorities, if he's asleep on a bed of leaves to be found by some jogger. They have no strength left but we have to keep going, they complain and say they want to stop, and every couple of steps, it's dad, where is he. Your dad stayed there camping and he'll catch up with us later on. They don't argue with me, or complain about having to walk. The displaced, fighters, the deported have run away feverish, sleepless, suffering from typhus, we're no better than them, OK? Are you two listening to me? We're no better than them and this isn't so bad, there are people who had to cut the hair off the women killed in the ovens. What ovens? Well, the ovens are another story, right now we have to keep walking fast, I can't carry them both at the same time, but they can carry one another, I don't have time right now to educate them. We aren't going to survive without a car, without food, but we always survive. We walk in single file along a shortcut and walk down to the water. We change the tickets, claiming we had problems with our flight, and board the boat without any issues. Perhaps he isn't dead, perhaps he just got up, went for a walk, and rebuilt his life. Perhaps they'll find him, but won't know who he is, nobody could say who he is, perhaps in ten years he'll remember we were hunting one another.

On the deck nobody pays any attention to us, I swing them in a hammock, we watch the coastline get further away, listen to the hoarse sound of the ship, the coastguard are on the lookout for a sinking ship in the countercurrent. Every now and then the siren whistles and we plunge into the depths of the ocean. We're nearly there, I can see the tip of the island, will there be dwarfs, elves, aliens, mom? We disembark with our hair flying in the wind and the skin of our faces parched, our lips dry from having drunk nothing for hours. Would you follow me to the end of the world? What's the end of the world? I can't teach you right now, just say yes, loving a mother is like joining a sect. Once we leave the boat I have to produce our documents, I don't know if they flag anything unusual but they let us continue towards the police checkpoint. We walk between glittering rocks, we are a black legend we are three crows. We walk over regular train tunnels and a service tunnel, all of them dug under the seabed. I take them to a little wooden house painted blue and white, bunk beds on old military train cars, turned into small restaurants for passersby. We order the shepherd's pie and a Cornish pasty. They watch the seagulls flying over the bluish boarded rooftops. They call these seagulls the terrors of Cornwall, the menace of the seas, they win the battle for the beaches in St. Ives, but they watch them and wave, they defend their innocence. We end lunch with a finale of colorful cakes covered in whipped cream when I spot men in uniform through the traditional windows. I can't remember when I got rid of the phone now, maybe it was on the main deck when nobody was watching. I still haven't heard anything, I don't know if I killed him, there's no television, there's nobody with a phone who could let me know, no witnesses, unless someone was hanging from one of the branches at that very moment. I'm not sure if my face gives me away, my non-English looks. We descend along the rocks between underground dwellings and drawbridges at the entrances to forts and castles. The sun doesn't make an appearance, but don't worry, the sun will have its revenge. How will the sun have its revenge? We talk about cold, deliberate vengeance and the stars, all the way back along the winding, thorny paths. I tell them honestly that, luckily, we will all be smashed to smithereens soon, within a thousand years, what difference does it make. The brothers, not understanding distress, become extremely distressed, they say one day the sun will stop warming us and everything will die out. Everything will die out, mom, an entire world crushed by stone-cold darkness, but then life will just be mountains of trash, mountains of moldy charcoal, of course boys! But we can't just give up and sink into despair, we're here! Ready for vengeance! We choose a hiding place to leave our possessions like vagrants, dirty T-shirts, stale bread, we can't carry these things anymore, we'll have to buy everything new. Everything new, everything new! There? We head off. Secularism disappeared off the face of the earth, I say out loud, but nobody understands me, nobody wants to understand.

The only available tickets are for tomorrow afternoon, all flights are fully booked to that destination, but why would anyone want to go there? And now? If he's dead, how long will it take for a tourist to discover him at their feet, raise the alarm, take him to forensics, all that cadaverous bureaucracy. But if he woke up alone in the brightness of the day, like a new man, like a bird, and started to wander through the coastal town, he could spot the stone at any moment and denounce me. Then, at this very moment, we would have a warrant out for my arrest on the runway. They could be accused of being potential accomplices, the boys with their little tray table unfolded, their earphones and their snacks. I choose a random chain hotel with an out of service swimming pool close to the airport, hidden behind tall grasses. We will go there and wait for the hours to pass by, with no surprises. In those hotels where people take revenge on their spouses before they hang themselves and leave their children under the bed wrapped up like packages. Congratulations, here in the hotel where we got married I leave you to what you deserve, you choose, burial or cremation. The cameras in the hallways show the comings and goings of the child-killers. The room is the same as any room in the Concordia, Rungis, Ibis, or B&B hotels. We take off our shoes, turn up the heat to the max, they're in their underpants, they turn on the television, we search for something in Spanish. We spend the day horizontal, stealing from the minifridge embedded in the wall, ordering room service using fake names, getting candy and snacks from the machine and looking out of the window at ambulances. In the evening they pass out sooner than expected. I cover them with synthetic blankets and walk in circles around the thirteen square meters.

Everything that followed the kidnapping of the twins was staged. Feasts, family walks along the Loire, feeding the ducks, going to buy the golden Christmas wrapping paper with the mother-in-law, going with the parents-in-law to the farm to watch the donkeys eat hay, but everything thrown off course by the image of my mother-

in-law cutting the wig and throwing locks of hair into the fire. The following week I spotted her within a block of the daycare pretending to be jogging and they even saw her on the other side of the fence, spying on the playground. Eventually I started locking the doors after they came back from school and I would watch them while they jumped on the trampoline or swung on the hammocks between the pine trees, but whenever I showered or took a nap I could hear them opening their windows to snatch the boys. This is when the mental escape began, the only one that counts, the advance and the retreat.

It's two o'clock, anxiety blooms, I sweat as the night progresses, I watch the airplanes skid, lower and retract their wheels. The amplified sound of the turbines, the men who look like they're dancing on the runway in their neon suits. I open the door, the DO NOT DISTURB sign, there's nobody in the hallway, there's a tray covered in leftover food outside one of the rooms. I take the card and the bathroom light turns off, the boys are submerged in an ocean of darkness. I walk over the colorful carpet, what can I do to wind down, in the lobby the employee confirms that everything nearby is closed, the massage parlor, the Vietnamese restaurants, the currency exchanges. Everything except, she says, but I doubt it, the Discothèque Rampard, the chain hotel's cabaret club, but I'm not sure you'd fit in, I'm not sure if it's for people your age. I walk past roundabouts, foreign construction businesses, the outside of an LDL, Nissan showrooms, and an electrical appliances chain. I walk without any personality. I cross a yard full of tow trucks, a swimming pool dealer, and next to a plant nursery I see the sign, Rampard. The bouncer looks at me but I always think everyone's looking at me funny, he must imagine I want to self-medicate in there, that I've come looking for easy money or for another chance at youth at the expense of these English scumbags. I'm here for a drink, I tell him, a drink before my flight, the bouncer doesn't give a shit if I come out of there alive and he pushes the curtain open for me. Inside it's the seventies, it's a hovel with standing copper ashtrays, smudged stripper poles, shiny colored lights, pool tables. I don't know anyone, but I feel like everyone is talking about me, are they? I didn't come prepared, my clothes are far too big, at a table in the corner three men eat grilled meat sandwiches and smoke cigars. My English is bad, but I can make myself understood although I'm not sure if they're making fun of me or telling jokes among themselves. I dance for a few songs and pass by close to their table, the men look at me, they laugh, I take a seat at the bar, what's the time?, I ask, like a confused tourist who's about to miss their flight. It's not late, I order two strong drinks, my stomach hurts, my head hurts, everything is spinning. I don't know if I'm pretending to be dizzy, I don't know if I'm pretending to be afraid of what's about to happen to me, what's going to happen to me, I don't know, but there's something hovering, a whiff in the air. Now I'm dancing to a Venezuelan reggaeton song close to their table, those three men.

One gestures at me to come closer, I look around, I don't see anyone else, I approach them. Are you talking to me? Are you alone? Nobody should be alone here, come here, come here with us so we can look after you, and he gets someone to bring him an extra chair. If the English police came in here demanding to see everyone's licenses I'd be better off sitting with these three. What do you want?, the one with green glasses asks me, the truth is I haven't had dinner, I say, bring this doll everything on the menu. I don't know if they're making fun of me by calling me doll, if they're messing with me in this psychedelic environment, someone comes out from behind the curtain and leaves several gold plates on the table. I eat with my hands, I don't have a napkin, I lick my fingers, I don't want to ask them anything, I don't want to reveal anything, I don't want them to make me talk. It seems I have to eat it all because they're still looking at me and they don't stop until I finish everything. They give me drinks, skinny young women dance around us, hanging from the poles, spinning around, only their crotches are visible, only their membranes, the openings, the orifices take center stage. The white cigarette smoke dissipates around the shiny leather boots of the three men who surround me. One of them helps me up, offering me his hand in a gentlemanly fashion, the other two follow him. They open the curtain and get me to walk through to the other side. I can still hear the reggaeton, I'm standing in a barely lit area in a greenish gloom with a curved sofa and I don't understand the situation, what's going to happen to me, what do they want me to do. What if they've been sent here? What if they're undercover French police? Did they give them all his savings hidden in the freezers? How much for the head of a white foreigner? One of them dances with me, I don't know how to move, he helps me move my hips, I don't know what the fuck I'm singing, I hear, *waaa, naaaa, dandandandan*, I repeat, *waaa, naaa, dandandandan*, I sway from side to side, he gives me something else to eat, I swallow it without knowing what it is. I let myself go, I'm a monkey, I'm a hostage in a prisoner exchange, they let my hair down. What if they take nude photos of me to send to the father? I know nothing, *naaa. Tatatata, mmmmm, wawawawawa.* They sit me down on the faux leather sofa and I dance for the three of them, I didn't know I was capable of opening myself up so wide, of provoking such arousal, of turning three men into animals. The shortest one lifts up my T-shirt and pulls my bra to one side, the three of them touch my breasts, suddenly I'm the only one with breasts in the entire regiment, suddenly I'm a source of pleasure for these murderous soldiers. I twerk on my knees leaning against the worn faux leather, between the burning, the ardor, and the fear I can't quite see their faces, I have one behind me, the other in front, they talk to each other, I don't understand what they're saying. They aren't aggressive, they get me to move like a cat, I close my eyes, I don't know anything, I didn't kill anyone, they touch me all over, they pull down my clothes, pull them aside, they break my shoulder strap, they pass me from one to the other, the songs take longer and longer to change. They give me something to drink straight from the bottle and the liquid runs down my body's tubes until it reaches my blood, I get carried away, I don't want them to think they are raping me and that I'm going to accuse them, I don't want to give them a reason to kill me. One of them pushes himself inside me, the tall one, I think, the other one is all over my stomach, he must be turned on by fat, he must be fantasizing about eating my fat, what time is it, I have to go, it's been fine but I want to go, I want to wash myself. Suddenly I'm bouncing on the small one's round stomach, for a moment I feel like I'm bouncing higher and higher on a theme park bouncy castle, I tell myself that my life is completely absurd. The roundabouts, the plant nursery, the domestic appliances place, the LDL, return with the magnetized card to the room, fly in a few hours. What if the owner of this dive has already alerted the French police and they're on their way disguised as pole dance patrons. Now I'm in the hands of the second one, I watch myself transform from femme fatale to terrified caged animal. The night crackles, sin surrounds us and sin always repeats itself, tatata, like shouting at god, give it to me, give it to me good with the vibrator on the clitoris, go on, crime is sticky. The three men get me to dance, I don't know anything about them, they talk to one another, one of them could be the son of a high-ranking state official, of an evangelical priest with a great reputation in Hackney, they touch each other too, they're more focused on one another than on me. I imagine that the tall one always wanted to please his father the priest, that he joined the British Armed Forces, tried to become an elite pilot to please him, but he failed, they kicked him out with no medals, his youth slipped through his fingertips. So he became a bouncer at a lousy cabaret club and every damn night he dreams about inviting his father to come and drink without paying a cent, he waits for him at the bar, serves him a glass of whiskey, his head red and fat, but his father never arrives. I stop moving, I try to pull up my shoulder strap, they don't let me, I see them, far too much evangelist TV, a crime against rabbits traumatized the kindhearted child, the sin, the rabbit traps scattered around the house, the child wants to get them out, the father shows no mercy. I manage to pull myself free, that's it, they don't want me to leave, between the three of them they grab me, they put me into fetal positions, scatological positions, I don't have to shout, I don't have to speak in another language, I don't have to ask for justice, that's the worst thing, asking for justice. You never know what it might awaken, hardly any crimes are avenged, why would they be. Above all, I don't want to raise the stakes, I don't want them to think they are abusers because that always infuriates and turns them on even more, the hatred is activated as soon as they're discovered. I slip away, I duck, I run behind the curtain naked. The music *wawawa nananan tatatata* excites bodies like pieces of meat at the top of greasy poles, just like the old tyrants wanted, their dream came true. I pull on my clothes and run out claiming I need to go to the toilet.

Keep going straight or turn? I decide to go towards an area of neon lights, I walk, I recognize the first roundabout, I'm not sure if I'm wasted or not, I see an imported car showroom, a construction shop, the outside of a LDL, these images seem familiar. I get back to the hotel like the dog left at the edge of the highway that travels hundreds of kilometers until it reaches the door of the family that abandoned it. I am astonished to find my hotel, I didn't think it was so close. A couple smokes outside the automatic doors, I follow them inside. I climb the service stairs, what floor are we on? I don't have a visual memory, all the doors look the same. I try the second floor, none of the door numbers seem like ours. I try the third, the fourth, but I don't recognize the door. Destroy the other as much as possible, an entire life spent signing fake checks, pretending to speak to clients on the telephone, an entire life going to and from an imaginary job, saying hello and goodbye but never leaving the simulation zone. If he got up after falling, I'd like to ask him if he loved me, but how would I know, he wouldn't know either even if he said yes, nobody fully realizes when they're lying. I press my ear to the door that I think is the right one, yes, it's that one, I look for the card, I lost it or they took it, I look under the crack to see if there's any light, or if they're crying, nothing. I gently knock, I call them. I go down to the lobby, there's nobody there. I climb back up the stairs again so the cameras don't see me. I knock on the door, worried I'll wake up the other guests, I knock harder, open up, open up, I whisper, it's mom, mom's here, I fall asleep on the carpet out in the hallway.

The first escape attempts were a fiasco. My parents-in-law walked arm-in-arm past the front door with the drug addict neighbors. Their awareness of reality and vision had begun to decline a while ago, but now everything had gotten worse and they were out of control. They saw me and smiled at me, incontinent, carnal. I'd set into motion my plan to whisk the boys away when the father-in-law untethered himself from the mother-in-law and came through the gate without my permission to help me with the engine. I slammed the hood shut and went inside to wait for the boyfriend's arrival. The other time was in the middle of the night, the sudden light in the parents-in-law's kitchen window like the stab of a knife and the shadow in a nightgown coming and going. Later, the written messages began to appear, little pieces of paper, graffiti, mysterious messages scrawled into the ground with my initials and a star of David.

The airport is like an improvised hospital set up during the epidemic. I'm wearing black sunglasses, my hangover is disguised, the smell scrubbed off. The boys opened the door with their eyes closed, I don't think anyone saw me spend the night in the hallway. Next to the security gates there are photos with descriptions of missing persons. Alarming disappearance. Audrey Baltrons. Forty years old. Mother of two children, eleven and twelve years old. Height, five four, short, brown hair, blue eyes, a tattoo on her right breast. Nearsighted in one eye. She left the town of Auzits on February thirteenth around two o'clock in the afternoon in a metallic Seat, license plate DL-669-NT. There was a car seat in the back. The driver's rearview mirror had been repaired with adhesive tape. Anyone who has seen her or can provide information relevant to the investigation call the regional headquarters of the Judicial Police and the police station, next to the numbers in red. The boys read the words if they were a magic spell and memorize them. The hope of finding Qifeng again, the little Chinese girl lost in a market close to a river in 1994 and found twenty-four years later. And a long list of kidnapped or missing women. In France, between forty and fifty thousand people go missing every year, the majority of them choose to disappear. The law states that adults have the right to be forgotten, the right to leave everything behind without an explanation, sometimes life is nothing more than a mistake. A mistake from start to finish and it must be put to an end. Only disturbing disappearances are investigated. Afterwards come the men and the dogs. Urgent calls for witnesses of the abduction scene, even if at the time they thought it was a demonstration of love. We get through security, they ask us to take off everything, sunglasses, woolly hat, boots, necklaces, everything could beep, anything could explode. The alarm goes off and I'm searched with my arms and legs spread out in a cross. The boys open their arms too. When we arrive, welcome Argentina, I tell them, even though you may not believe it, you are both Argentine, here we are, nobody will find you here. Nothing out of the ordinary happens at the computers in customs, national customs director, general administration manager, customs operations manager, nobody intercepts us, nobody asks us to step into a white room to search our intestines, gall bladder, and rectum with a scanner. Something happens just as we are about to walk through the door towards the arrivals hall. Between the candy and magazine stalls I notice something without knowing exactly what it is. A police officer in civilian clothes says something into a walkie-talkie, another looks from left to right and nods towards the officer at the door. But what's really happening, what orders were given, how am I supposed to act in these situations, I try to think fast. We go into a pharmacy, it's not the best moment to walk through the exit door. We examine the brews, concoctions, infusions, potions, the employee wearing a white uniform asks me what I'm looking for. I take a liver medication from the shelf. But you need a prescription for that, madam. I see one of the boys collecting throat lozenges as though they were wild mushrooms. Sorry, I tell her, I'm not from here you see. The brothers play, they're wasps and bumblebees bumping against the glass, passing by outside are agents escorted by guards and other corrupt customs officials in charge of border crossings. We hide behind the palliative care shelves. There's nothing more we can do, escaping an airport is unthinkable so the three of us stay huddled down amongst the medicines, imitating indecisive sick people, until we hear the sound of pebbles hitting against the roof of the new terminal, followed by the boom of thunder. The shower of debris gets louder, the police at the doors move elsewhere. People look up at the aerial disaster, car alarms go off, we exit with our necks sunk down into our chests and emerge among the taxis and hired cars.

The brothers fall asleep instantly, blocking out the world around them and burrowing inside themselves like Asian pangolins. The driver watches television. I open and close my eyes to see the highway and the billboards thuggish propaganda and electoral advertisements. Just like back there, the State regulates minors here, their sale, purchase, private parties, and the unbridled enjoyment of their precocious bodies. We arrive in the capital, the boys wake up in Balvanera as we cross Plaza Miserere, the shoes hanging from the telephone wires, everything seems like a movie to them. We get out at a small square close to the train station, is this a barrio? Yes, it's called a barrio. The poor things exist outside of society, they'll never integrate. We enter the cool hallway of a building from the seventies, the boys throw themselves down onto the cold tile floor. We go up in an old elevator with wrought iron bars, the brothers think it looks like a lion taming cage. We look like three caged creatures at an illegal circus and we laugh, the abandoned animals run in all directions, crashing into each other after a raid. I find the key and the little bundle of cash under the carpet, like they promised me, no notes, no calls, everything nameless.

You have parents too?, they ask. My childhood apartment has orange curtains, a few bedrooms, an old bathroom, a refrigerator with a bag of milk and two apples. The brothers are lost, they don't sit down, they don't lie down, they don't walk, they don't fight, I only know they have a pulse because they're standing up. You used to live here? We go into my room and the three of us throw ourselves onto my bed, one on top of the other, everything is exactly how it was when I was young, they boys touch the objects, the camera, books, like an exhibition showing the house of a deported woman, the guided visit to the dead woman's bedroom with translations into various languages. It swiftly gets dark. We were looking up at the sky when everything vanished. Does it get dark faster here, mom? I think it does, I think everything happens faster. The clouds, the rain, the westerly wind, the sunset.

Shall we go down to look around? We walk through the neighborhood, we come across a costume shop with raised shutters. We walk inside, it's as long as a prison courtyard, at the end there's a man working on a rabbit costume with white, hard eyes. The boys want to try it on, the man finishes sticking on the shiny white eyes with superglue and blows on them. When it's dry I can show them how it looks. Yes, they shout and walk carefully between the costumes strung up like dinner guests hung half a meter from the ground. I look towards the street, a few people pass by with a cart filled with trash, a workhorse leans down to try and drink water from the drain but his load is too heavy, a man with the face of an informant takes a drag of a cigarette and flicks it away, there's no escape even in my childhood barrio. The brothers are now two albino rabbits that escaped from their pen and are chasing me, like the albino rabbits that my father-in-law would kill in front of my husband. The man gives them a fake ax and a black carrot for them to terrorize me with. I watch them look for me and I hide in an aisle behind a devil costume.

We put on baseball caps, we buy tropical sandals and white sleeveless shirts from a street vendor, we take off our scruffy winter clothes then and there. One day passes, exactly the same as the next, we remain adrift in that apartment with the orange curtains, no contact with the neighbors or with anyone else, at night we go out to watch the metal shutters slamming down like guillotines, we like watching how the streets are emptied of boxes, bags, and tons of food and how the trains stop in their tracks. Sometimes we patiently wait for McDonald's to close and they give us the leftover food so we don't need to stick our arms into the trash container. That man looks like dad and that one too and that man sleeping against the subway barrier, could they all be dad? We like eating hot dogs with fried onions standing up, we like the neighborhood ice cream parlors and their fantastical creations. We find a shopping mall and the brothers we baptized J and E climb atop a horse screwed onto a wooden frame that has been made to look like a cactus. It's coin operated, I insert one, the horse moves, I lift J onto it, we watch him ride across the plains of the northeast and Mesopotamia, J gets bored, I lift him off, the horse keeps galloping, I lift up E. But the horse keeps going and E gets bored of the western plains too. I get the feeling that I saved two lives, it may not mean much to the nation's decorated heroes but it's better than nothing and there will always be those who cover up a crime by making it look like an accident and there will always be cynics. I watch them playing in a square around the vertical streams of water and the old merry-go-rounds. It's been days now and no news, in public the order is not to speak much, if someone asks us for the time, we don't respond. Another day, sleep, change money at a black-market exchange, walk around naked, buy fake designer shorts, ankle socks, canvas sneakers, patriotic caps, shave their heads so they both transform into pale birds. Just like being cheated on, we want to see the images up close, was it face down, face up, I wonder where he is now, what he's doing, what's the look on his face, did he get up, did his head stay there. I wonder if he took the same ferry, following in our footsteps and he's only a few meters behind us. Just in case, I have no phone, I don't set foot in a phone booth, I don't utter the names of my parents or my brother in front of them.

In a bar with pool tables and pinball machines I watch on TV a news story about women who've been burned and had their throats cut, plain old murder has gone out of fashion, now torture is essential, the drunkard's cloak, the brazen bull, the thumbscrew, the rack, the Judas cradle, the iron maiden, anything medieval is all the rage. The brothers eat mashed potatoes. They love the food, they can't believe it, the diners watch television, Susan, who was married to David Smith, had an extramarital affair with a man who ended their relationship with a letter that explained that the essential problem of their relationship was her kids. Smith started to hate her children, leading her to murder them on the night of the October 25, 1994. That night, Smith put the children in the back of the family car and drove to a dirt road on the edge of a lake. She parked the car on a cliffside and removed the handbrake. The car sank with the children still inside, who drowned. She was given a prison sentence of thirty years to life on the July 27, 1995. She will have a chance at parole in November 2024. She'll be out soon, she'll be among us, going to cabarets, having more children or who knows what. The boys lick the salt off their plates and want more bread. Bread, bread! There's a desire for destruction in the human heart, it's so large, so towering, so convinced that nothing can stop it, but anyway, let's raise our glasses, here we are little brothers, there are worse lives than ours, almost all lives are worse than those of three fugitives.

We walk along Avenida Pueyrredón and turn at Pasteur, I take them into the half light of a synagogue. I take them all the way to the lectern, the three of us gaze in silence at the wooden seats engraved with surnames. They don't understand what this place is, what we're doing here. I can see entire generations sitting on these very benches, year after year, the Kaddish for the dead, human madness, a man kicks us out because we're on the wrong side of the synagogue, there's still a whiff of the fast hanging in the air. We walk down Calle Junín, we turn onto Lavalle, it's like walking arm in arm on the grounds of an asylum, very far away from the world, drugged, calm, submerged. They search for things on the street, bits of Chinese toys, they're handed balloons with the name of a Peruvian restaurant, they adapt to being two rosy-cheeked boys with shaved heads and not speaking in public, behind closed doors they practice the R, vowels, the facial expressions they must make and how much to open their mouths. Where is your family? they ask, but we can't see them yet, they will come to us, we will have a house, would you like a tree house, close to the waterfalls? Argentina is very large, they could never find anyone here, even if they sent secret agents. A red-headed woman gestures at me, and keeps walking, it's my mother, I'm almost certain, I turn around to watch her, she is walking fast but it's her, I know it is.

We're distracted and have almost arrived home with our shopping when I see a poster stuck to the Precinct 11 Police Station. REWARD LISA TREJMAN USD 10,000 seeking information on the whereabouts of a mother and sons, wanted by Interpol. Lisa Trejman, born 18/11/1976, Argentine and Polish dual nationality, Argentine ID number 26.282.139, has been sentenced to prison in France for the kidnapping of her twin sons Jonay and Elías Fournier, of French and Argentine nationalities, born on 13/03/2018. Armand Fournier's paternal family who reside in France will award an immediate payment of 10,000 USD for any information leading to the capture of Lisa Trejman and the children, Jonay Fournier and Elías Fournier, approximately five years of age. It's very likely that the mother and her children are living under assumed identities, with altered hairstyles, and that the story they tell will differ from the criminal facts. If you see a woman with two children who appear to be identical twins but are nonidentical, that match the photos and find it difficult to speak the local language, please get in touch. Lisa Trejman has a mother and a father who live in Buenos Aires but whose current whereabouts are unknown, apparently she has not contacted them in order to protect them, and has a brother with no fixed address who calls himself a singer, lost in a coastal region between Argentina and Uruguay. Their homes have been raided and the information obtained is being closely studied, but no incriminating evidence has been recovered yet. They could be in Argentina or elsewhere, but they can't hide forever. Interpol France, the entire European Union, and the rest of the world have emitted a red alert. A guaranteed prison sentence awaits her. The children are in danger as long as they are with their mother. The kidnapper's mother's family have firm roots in the Jewish community so there is a chance that they are helping her, unaware of Lisa Trejman's criminal background as a kidnapping mother. Jewish institutions and synagogues could be raided. Lisa Trejman is a criminal and must go to prison. We have hundreds of testimonies from residents of the French village about the abductor in question. The boys' paternal grandparents have hired experts in cases for children kidnapped by their own parents, who requested we publish this notice. Please contact our office with any information at info@galois.com and +5491118111503, we will evaluate the information provided and if it leads to the capture of the mother and the rescue of the children you will receive a reward. Courts of record: Fifth Criminal Court of Argentina, Thirteenth National Criminal and Correctional Court. File: 22012/2021 Bourges Appeals Court 10 correctional chamber Record: 54/2032 Prosecutor: 22264000193.

We had gone down into the catacombs to explore the underground world and see the stalactites, the green water, the floating skulls, when we began to hear the sound of the flood. The babies were in the family home with the parents-in-law, the water was rising up the narrow channels much faster than we expected. We didn't see anyone else, we had very little time left, we had to decide whether to move and find the exit or stay still so the rocky wall wouldn't crumble, but we didn't know how high the water would climb. Breathing was almost impossible, we could feel we had very little precious time left, that our orphaned children would be raised by others, and that we had an alliance: he was the fuse, and I was the match.

It gets dark, we are no longer within his reach. I fought to have them with me but ever since before they were born they only ever served one end, the tragic end of lovers.

New Directions Paperbooks—a partial listing

Adonis, Songs of Mihyar the Damascene
César Aira, Ghosts
An Episode in the Life of a Landscape Painter
Ryunosuke Akutagawa, Kappa
Will Alexander, Refractive Africa
Osama Alomar, The Teeth of the Comb
Guillaume Apollinaire, Selected Writings
Jessica Au, Cold Enough for Snow
Paul Auster, The Red Notebook
Ingeborg Bachmann, Malina
Honoré de Balzac, Colonel Chabert
Djuna Barnes, Nightwood
Charles Baudelaire, The Flowers of Evil*
Bei Dao, City Gate, Open Up
Yevgenia Belorusets, Lucky Breaks
Rafael Bernal, His Name Was Death
Mei-Mei Berssenbrugge, Empathy
Max Blecher, Adventures in Immediate Irreality
Jorge Luis Borges, Labyrinths
Seven Nights
Coral Bracho, Firefly Under the Tongue*
Kamau Brathwaite, Ancestors
Anne Carson, Glass, Irony & God
Wrong Norma
Horacio Castellanos Moya, Senselessness
Camilo José Cela, Mazurka for Two Dead Men
Louis-Ferdinand Céline
Death on the Installment Plan
Journey to the End of the Night
Inger Christensen, alphabet
Julio Cortázar, Cronopios and Famas
Jonathan Creasy (ed.), Black Mountain Poems
Robert Creeley, If I Were Writing This
H.D., Selected Poems
Guy Davenport, 7 Greeks
Amparo Dávila, The Houseguest
Osamu Dazai, The Flowers of Buffoonery
No Longer Human
The Setting Sun
Anne de Marcken
It Lasts Forever and Then It's Over
Helen DeWitt, The Last Samurai
Some Trick
José Donoso, The Obscene Bird of Night
Robert Duncan, Selected Poems
Eça de Queirós, The Maias
Juan Emar, Yesterday
William Empson, 7 Types of Ambiguity
Mathias Énard, Compass
Shusaku Endo, Deep River
Jenny Erpenbeck, Go, Went, Gone
Kairos
Lawrence Ferlinghetti
A Coney Island of the Mind
Thalia Field, Personhood
F. Scott Fitzgerald, The Crack-Up
Rivka Galchen, Little Labors
Forrest Gander, Be With
Romain Gary, The Kites
Natalia Ginzburg, The Dry Heart
Henry Green, Concluding
Marlen Haushofer, The Wall
Victor Heringer, The Love of Singular Men
Felisberto Hernández, Piano Stories
Hermann Hesse, Siddhartha
Takashi Hiraide, The Guest Cat
Yoel Hoffmann, Moods
Susan Howe, My Emily Dickinson
Concordance
Bohumil Hrabal, I Served the King of England
Qurratulain Hyder, River of Fire
Sonallah Ibrahim, That Smell
Rachel Ingalls, Mrs. Caliban
Christopher Isherwood, The Berlin Stories
Fleur Jaeggy, Sweet Days of Discipline
Alfred Jarry, Ubu Roi
B.S. Johnson, House Mother Normal
James Joyce, Stephen Hero
Franz Kafka, Amerika: The Man Who Disappeared
Yasunari Kawabata, Dandelions
Mieko Kanai, Mild Vertigo
John Keene, Counternarratives
Kim Hyesoon, Autobiography of Death
Heinrich von Kleist, Michael Kohlhaas
Taeko Kono, Toddler-Hunting
László Krasznahorkai, Satantango
Seiobo There Below
Ágota Kristóf, The Illiterate
Eka Kurniawan, Beauty Is a Wound
Mme. de Lafayette, The Princess of Clèves
Lautréamont, Maldoror
Siegfried Lenz, The German Lesson
Alexander Lernet-Holenia, Count Luna

Denise Levertov, Selected Poems
Li Po, Selected Poems
Clarice Lispector, An Apprenticeship
The Hour of the Star
The Passion According to G. H.
Federico García Lorca, Selected Poems*
Nathaniel Mackey, Splay Anthem
Xavier de Maistre, Voyage Around My Room
Stéphane Mallarmé, Selected Poetry and Prose*
Javier Marías, Your Face Tomorrow (3 volumes)
Bernadette Mayer, Midwinter Day
Carson McCullers, The Member of the Wedding
Fernando Melchor, Hurricane Season
Paradais
Thomas Merton, New Seeds of Contemplation
The Way of Chuang Tzu
Henri Michaux, A Barbarian in Asia
Henry Miller, The Colossus of Maroussi
Big Sur & the Oranges of Hieronymus Bosch
Yukio Mishima, Confessions of a Mask
Death in Midsummer
Eugenio Montale, Selected Poems*
Vladimir Nabokov, Laughter in the Dark
Pablo Neruda, The Captain's Verses*
Love Poems*
Charles Olson, Selected Writings
George Oppen, New Collected Poems
Wilfred Owen, Collected Poems
Hiroko Oyamada, The Hole
José Emilio Pacheco, Battles in the Desert
Michael Palmer, Little Elegies for Sister Satan
Nicanor Parra, Antipoems*
Boris Pasternak, Safe Conduct
Octavio Paz, Poems of Octavio Paz
Victor Pelevin, Omon Ra
Fernando Pessoa
The Complete Works of Alberto Caeiro
Alejandra Pizarnik
Extracting the Stone of Madness
Robert Plunket, My Search for Warren Harding
Ezra Pound, The Cantos
New Selected Poems and Translations
Qian Zhongshu, Fortress Besieged
Raymond Queneau, Exercises in Style
Olga Ravn, The Employees
Herbert Read, The Green Child
Kenneth Rexroth, Selected Poems
Keith Ridgway, A Shock
Rainer Maria Rilke
Poems from the Book of Hours
Arthur Rimbaud, Illuminations*
A Season in Hell and The Drunken Boat*
Evelio Rosero, The Armies
Fran Ross, Oreo
Joseph Roth, The Emperor's Tomb
Raymond Roussel, Locus Solus
Ihara Saikaku, The Life of an Amorous Woman
Nathalie Sarraute, Tropisms
Jean-Paul Sartre, Nausea
Kathryn Scanlan, Kick the Latch
Delmore Schwartz
In Dreams Begin Responsibilities
W. G. Sebald, The Emigrants
The Rings of Saturn
Anne Serre, The Governesses
Patti Smith, Woolgathering
Stevie Smith, Best Poems
Novel on Yellow Paper
Gary Snyder, Turtle Island
Muriel Spark, The Driver's Seat
The Public Image
Maria Stepanova, In Memory of Memory
Wislawa Szymborska, How to Start Writing
Antonio Tabucchi, Pereira Maintains
Junichiro Tanizaki, The Maids
Yoko Tawada, The Emissary
Scattered All over the Earth
Dylan Thomas, A Child's Christmas in Wales
Collected Poems
Thuan, Chinatown
Rosemary Tonks, The Bloater
Tomas Tranströmer, The Great Enigma
Leonid Tsypkin, Summer in Baden-Baden
Tu Fu, Selected Poems
Elio Vittorini, Conversations in Sicily
Rosmarie Waldrop, The Nick of Time
Robert Walser, The Tanners
Eliot Weinberger, An Elemental Thing
Nineteen Ways of Looking at Wang Wei
Nathanael West, The Day of the Locust
Miss Lonelyhearts
Tennessee Williams, The Glass Menagerie
A Streetcar Named Desire
William Carlos Williams, Selected Poems
Alexis Wright, Praiseworthy
Louis Zukofsky, "A"

*BILINGUAL EDITION

For a complete listing, request a free catalog from New Directions, 80 8th Avenue, New York, NY 10011
or visit us online at **ndbooks.com**